CW01019840

SPACE: 1999
ROGUE PLANET

by

E. C. Tubb

Published by Powys Books

Los Angeles, California, USA

First Powys Books Printing: November 2019

        10 9 8 7 6 5 4 3 2 1

ISBN-13: 978-1-7334561-0-4

Powys Media
Buena Park, CA 90620

www.powysmedia.com

Books by E. C. Tubb:

The Dumarest Saga (US: Dumarest of Terra)

1. *The Winds of Gath* (1967) (also published with slightly modified text as *Gath* [1968, 2010])
2. *Derai* (1968) (also published as *The Death Zone* [2010])
3. *Toyman* (1969)
4. *Kalin* (1969)
5. *The Jester at Scar* (1970)
6. *Lallia* (1971)
7. *Technos* (1972)
8. *Veruchia* (1973)
9. *Mayenne* (1973)
10. *Jondelle* (1973)
11. *Zenya* (1974)
12. *Eloise* (1975)
13. *Eye of the Zodiac* (1975)
14. *Jack of Swords* (1976)
15. *Spectrum of a Forgotten Sun* (1976)
16. *Haven of Darkness* (1977)
17. *Prison of Night* (1977)
18. *Incident on Ath* (1978)
19. *The Quillian Sector* (1978)
20. *Web of Sand* (1979)
21. *Iduna's Universe* (1979)
22. *The Terra Data* (1980)
23. *World of Promise* (1980)
24. *Nectar of Heaven* (1981)
25. *The Terridae* (1981)
26. *The Coming Event* (1982)

Cap Kennedy (UK: F.A.T.E.)

All as by Gregory Kern

1. *Galaxy of the Lost* (1973)
2. *Slave Ship from Sergan* (1973)
3. *Monster of Metelaze* (1973)
4. *Enemy Within the Skull* (1974)
5. *Jewel of Jarhen* (1974)
6. *Seetee Alert!* (1974)
7. *The Gholan Gate* (1974)
8. *The Eater of Worlds* (1974)
9. *Earth Enslaved* (1974)
10. *Planet of Dread* (1974)
11. *Spawn of Laban* (1974)
12. *The Genetic Buccaneer* (1974)
13. *A World Aflame* (1974)
14. *The Ghosts of Epidoris* (1975)
15. *Mimics of Dephene* (1975)
16. *Beyond the Galactic Lens* (1975)
17. *The Galactiad* (1983) (written 1976 but previously only published in German language as *Das kosmische Duell* [1976])

Space: 1999

1. *Breakaway* (1975)
2. *Collision Course* (1975)
3. *Alien Seed* (1976)
4. *Rogue Planet* (1976) (also published in a revised edition [2019])

5. *Earthfall* (1977) (also published in 25th anniversary revised edition [2002])
6. *Earthbound* (2003)

The Chronicles of Malkar

1. *Death God's Doom* (1999)
2. *The Sleeping City* (1999)

Other science fiction novels

Tubb's 1954 novel *The Resurrected Man* saw its first American publication as the cover story on the December 1958 issue of Satellite Science Fiction

- *Saturn Patrol* (1951), as by King Lang
  - also published as *Saturn Patrol* (1996) by E.C. Tubb
- *Planetfall* (1951), as by Gill Hunt
- *Argentis* (1952), as by Brian Shaw
  - also published as *Argentis* (1979) by E.C. Tubb
- *Alien Impact* (1952)
- *Alien Universe* (1952), as by Volsted Gridban
  - also published as *The Green Helix* (2009) by E.C. Tubb
- *Reverse Universe* (1952), as by Volsted Gridban
- *Atom War on Mars* (1952)
- *Planetoid Disposals Ltd.* (1953), as by Volsted Gridban
- *De Bracy's Drug* (1953), as by Volsted Gridban

- o also published as *De Bracy's Drug* (2004) by E.C. Tubb
- o also published as *The Freedom Army* (2009) by E.C. Tubb
- *Fugitive of Time* (1953), as by Volsted Gridban
- *The Wall* (1953), as by Charles Grey
  - o also published as *The Wall* (1999, 2009) by E.C. Tubb
- *The Mutants Rebel* (1953)
  - o also published as *World in Torment* (2008)
- *Dynasty of Doom* (1953), as by Charles Grey
- *The Tormented City* (1953), as by Charles Grey
  - o also published as *Secret of the Towers* (2008) by E.C. Tubb
- *Space Hunger* (1953), as by Charles Grey
  - o also published as *Earth Set Free* (1999) by E.C. Tubb
  - o also published as *The Price of Freedom* (2008) by E.C. Tubb
- *I Fight for Mars* (1953), as by Charles Grey
  - o also published as *I Fight for Mars* (1998) by E.C. Tubb
- *Venusian Adventure* (1953)
- *Alien Life* (1954)
- *The Living World* (1954), as by Carl Maddox
- *The Extra Man* (1954)
  - o also published as *Fifty Days to Doom* (2010)
- *Menace from the Past* (1954), as by Carl Maddox
- *The Metal Eater* (1954), as by Roy Sheldon

- *Journey to Mars* (1954)
- *World at Bay* (1954)
  - also published as *Tide of Death* (2008)
- *City of No Return* (1954)
- *Hell Planet* (1954)
- *The Resurrected Man* (1954)
- *The Stellar Legion* (1954)
- *The Hand of Havoc* (1954), as by Charles Grey
- *Enterprise 2115* (1954), as by Charles Grey
  - also published as *The Mechanical Monarch* (1958) by E.C. Tubb
- *Alien Dust* (1955)
- *The Space-Born* (1956)
- *Touch of Evil* (1957), as by Arthur Maclean
  - also published in revised version as *The Possessed* (2005) by E.C. Tubb
- *Moon Base* (1964)
- *Death is a Dream* (1967)
- *The Life-Buyer* (1967)
  - also published as *The Life Buyer* (2006)
- *C.O.D. - Mars* (1968)
  - also published as *Fear of Strangers* (2007)
- *Escape into Space* (1969)
- *S.T.A.R. Flight* (1969)
- *Century of the Manikin* (1972)
- *The Primitive* (1977)
- *Death Wears a White Face* (1979)
  - also published as *Dead Weight* (2007)
- *Stellar Assignment* (1979)
- *The Luck Machine* (1980)
- *Pawn of the Omphalos* (1980)

- o also published in revised version as
  Death God's Doom (1999)
- *Stardeath* (1983)
- *Pandora's Box* (1996) (previously unpublished
  work written 1954)
- *Temple of Death* (1996) (previously un-
  published work written 1954)
- *Alien Life* (1998) (revised and expanded version
  of *Alien Life* [1954])
  - o also published as *Journey into Terror*
    (2009)
- *Alien Worlds* (1999) (collection of *Alien Dust*
  [1955] and *Alien Universe* [1952])
- *Footsteps of Angels* (2004) (previously un-
  published work written c.1988)
- *Starslave* (2010) (previously unpublished work
  written 1984)
- *To Dream Again* (2011)
- *Fires of Satan* (2012)

Short story collections

- *Supernatural Stories 9* (1957), as by various
  pseudonyms
- *Ten from Tomorrow* (1966)
- *A Scatter of Stardust* (1972)
- *Kalgan the Golden* (1996)
- *Murder in Space* (1997)
- *The Best Science Fiction of E.C. Tubb* (2003)
- *Mirror of the Night and Other Weird Tales*
  (2003)

- *The Wager: Science Fiction Mystery Tales* (2011)
- *The Ming Vase and Other Science Fiction Stories* (2011)
- *Enemy of the State: Fantastic Mystery Stories* (2011)
- *Tomorrow: Science Fiction Mystery Tales* (2011)
- *The Wonderful Day: Science Fiction Stories* (2012)
- *Only One Winner: Science Fiction Mystery Tales* (2013)

Novellas

- *Freight* (1953, *Nebula* 3)
- *Subtle Victory* (1953, *Authentic Science Fiction* 39)
- *The Inevitable Conflict* (1954, *Vargo Statten Science Fiction* 1-3)
- *Forbidden Fruit* (1954, *Vargo Statten/British Science Fiction* 4-6)
- *Star Haven* (1954, *Authentic Science Fiction* 52)
- *Number Thirteen* (1956, *Authentic Science Fiction* 69), as by Douglas West
- *The Big Secret* (1956, *Authentic Science Fiction* 70), as by Ken Wainwright
- *The Give-Away Worlds* (1956, *Authentic Science Fiction* 72), as by Julian Cary
- *Enemy of the State* (1956, *Authentic Science Fiction* 74), as by Ken Wainwright

- *There's Only One Winner* (1957, *Authentic Science Fiction* 81), as by Nigel Lloyd
- *The Touch of Reality* (1958, *Nebula* 28)
- *Galactic Destiny* (1959, *SF Adventures* 10)
- *Spawn of Jupiter* (1970, *Vision of Tomorrow 11*)

Non-SF novels

- *Assignment New York* (1955), as by Mike Lantry
    - also published as *Assignment New York* (1996) by E.C. Tubb
- *The Fighting Fury* (1955), as by Paul Schofield
    - also published as *The Fighting Fury* (1962), as by Chuck Adams
    - also published as *The Gold Seekers* (2000) by E.C. Tubb
- *Comanche Capture* (1955), as by E. F. Jackson
    - also published as *The Captive* (2000), as by E.F. Jackson
    - also published as *The Captive* (2010) by E.C. Tubb
- *Sands of Destiny* (1955), as by Jud Cary
    - also published as *Sands of Destiny* (2009) by E.C. Tubb
    - also published as *Sands of Destiny: A Novel of the French Foreign Legion* (2011) by E.C. Tubb
- *Men of the Long Rifle* (1955), as by J.F. Clarkson

- o also published as *The Pathfinders* (2000), as by Charles Grey
- *Scourge of the South* (1956), as by M.L. Powers
  - o also published as *The Marauders* (1960), as by M.L. Powers
  - o also published as *Scourge of the South* (2000), as by George Holt
- *Vengeance Trail* (1956), as by James Farrow
  - o also published as *The Liberators* (2000), as by Brett Landry
- *Trail Blazers* (1956), as by Chuck Adams
  - o also published as *The Last Outlaw* (1961), as by Chuck Adams
  - o also published as *Trail Blazers* (2000), as by Eric Storm
  - o also published as *Trail Blazers* (2007) by E.C. Tubb
- *Quest for Quantrell* (1956), as by John Stevens
  - o also published as *Night Raiders* (1960), as by John Stevens
  - o also published as *Curse of Quantrill* (2000), as by Carl Maddox
- *Drums of the Prairie* (1956), as by P. Lawrence
  - o also published as *The Red Lance* (1959), as by L.P. Eastern
  - o also published as *The Dying Tree* (2000), as by Edward Thomson
- *Men of the West* (1956), as by Chet Lawson
  - o also published as *Massacre Trail* (1960), as by Chuck Adams
  - o also published as *Hills of Blood* (2000), as by Frank Weight
- *Wagon Trail* (1957), as by Charles S. Graham

- also published as *Cauldron of Violence* (2000), as by Gordon Kent
- also published as *Cauldron of Violence* (2010) by E.C. Tubb
- *Colt Vengeance* (1957), as by James R. Fenner
  - also published as *Colt Law* (1962), as by Chuck Adams
  - also published as *The First Shot* (2000) by E.C. Tubb

The Gladiators

All as by Edward Thomson

1. *Atilus the Slave* (1975)
2. *Atilus the Gladiator* (1975)
3. *Gladiator* (1978)

Comic Books

- *Hellfire Landing* (*Commando* issue 5, 1961)
- *Target Death* (*Combat Library* issue 102, 1961)
- *Lucky Strike* (*War Picture Library* issue 124, 1961)
- *Calculated Risk* (*Air Ace Picture Library* issue 78, 1961)
- *Too Tough to Handle* (*War Picture Library* issue 134, 1962)
- *The Dead Keep Faith* (*War Picture Library* issue 140, 1962)
- *The Spark of Anger* (*Battle Picture Library* issue 52, 1962)

- *Full Impact* (*Air Ace Picture Library* issue 92, 1962)
- *I Vow Vengeance* (*War at Sea Picture Library* issue 7, 1962)
- *One Must Die* (*Battle Picture Library* issue 72, 1962)
- *Gunflash* (*War Picture Library* issue 157, 1962)
- *Hit Back* (*Battle Picture Library* issue 69, 1962)
- *Suicide Squad* (*War Picture Library* issue 172, 1962)
- *No Higher Stakes* (*Battle Picture Library* issue 89, 1963)
- *Penalty of Fear* (*Thriller Picture Library* issue 444, 1963)

Anthologies

- *Gateway to the Stars* (ed. John Carnell, 1955) - 'Unfortunate Purchase'
- *SF: The Year's Greatest Science Fiction and Fantasy* (ed. Judith Merril, 1956) - 'The Last Day of Summer'
- *SF '59: The Year's Greatest Science Fiction and Fantasy* (ed. Judith Merril, 1959) - 'Fresh Guy'
- *The Vampire* (ed. Ornella Volta and Valerio Riva, 1963) - 'Fresh Guy'
- *The Year's Best SF: 9* (ed. Judith Merril, 1964) - 'The Ming Vase'
- *Dimension 4* (ed. Groff Conklin, 1964) - 'Sense of Proportion'
- *Best of New Worlds* (ed. Michael Moorcock, 1965) - 'New Experience'

- *Weird Shadows from Beyond* (ed. John Carnell, 1965) - 'Fresh Guy'
- *New Writings in SF 6* (ed. John Carnell, 1965) - 'The Seekers'
- *The Year's Best SF: 11th* (ed. Judith Merril, 1966) - 'J is for Jeanne'
- *SF Reprise 1* (ed. Michael Moorcock, 1966) - 'New Experience'
- *Window on the Future* (ed. Douglas Hill, 1966) - 'Sense of Proportion'
- *9th Annual S-F* (ed. Judith Merril, 1967) - 'The Ming Vase'
- *The Devil His Due* (ed. Douglas Hill, 1967) - 'Return Visit'
- *More Tales of Unease* (ed. John Burke, 1969) - 'Little Girl Lost'
- *The Best of Sci-fi 12* (ed. Judith Merril, 1970) - 'J is for Jeanne'
- *The Year's Best Horror Stories* (ed. Richard Davis, 1971) - 'Lucifer!'
- *New Writings in Horror and the Supernatural* (ed. David Sutton, 1971) - 'The Winner'
- *New Writings in SF 22* (ed. Kenneth Bulmer, 1973) - 'Evane'
- *Space 1* (ed. Richard Davis, 1973) - 'Mistaken Identity'
- *The 1974 Annual World's Best SF* (ed. Donald Wollheim, 1974) - 'Evane'
- *New Writings in SF 23* (ed. Kenneth Bulmer,1974) - 'Made to be Broken', 'Accolade'
- *History of the Science Fiction Magazine 1946-1955* (ed. Mike Ashley, 1974) - 'The Wager'

- *World's Best SF Short Stories 1* (ed. Donald Wollheim, 1975) - 'Evane'
- *New Writings in SF 28* (ed. Kenneth Bulmer, 1976) - 'Face to Infinity'
- *New Writings in SF 29* (ed. Kenneth Bulmer, 1976) - 'Random Sample'
- *Best of British SF Vol. 2* (ed. Mike Ashley, 1977) - 'Trojan Horse'
- *Strange Planets* (ed. A. Williams-Ellis and M. Pearson, 1977) - 'Made to be Broken'
- *New Writings in SF 30* (ed. Kenneth Bulmer, 1978) - 'Read Me This Riddle'
- *Perilous Planets* (ed. Brian Aldiss, 1978) - 'The Seekers'
- *The Androids Are Coming* (ed. Robert Silverberg, 1979) - 'The Captain's Dog'
- *Wollheim's World of Best SF* (ed. Donald Wollheim, 1979) - 'Evane'
- *Heroic Fantasy* (ed. Gerald Page and Hank Reinhardt, 1979) - 'Blood in the Mist'
- *Pulsar 2* (ed. George Hay, 1979) - 'The Knife'
- *Jewels of Wonder* (ed. Mike Ashley, 1981) - 'Blood in the Mist'
- *The Drabble Project* (ed. Rob Meades and David B Wake, 1988) - 'As it Really Was', 'The Very Small Knife'
- *Space Stories* (ed. Mike Ashley, 1996) - 'The Bells of Acheron'
- *Classical Stories: Heroic Tales from Ancient Greece and Rome* (ed. Mike Ashley, 1996) - 'The Sword of Freedom'

- *The New Random House Book of Science Fiction Stories* (ed. Mike Ashley, 1997) - 'The Bells of Acheron'
- *Fantasy Annual 1* (ed. Philip Harbottle and Sean Wallace, 1997) - 'Time and Again'
- *Heroic Adventure Stories: From the Golden Age of Greece and Rome* (ed. Mike Ashley, 1998) - 'The Sword of Freedom'
- *Giant Book of Heroic Adventure Stories* (ed. Mike Ashley, 1998) - 'The Sword of Freedom'
- *The Iron God/Tomorrow* Gryphon Double (ed. Philip Harbottle, 1998) - 'Tomorrow'
- *Fantasy Annual 2* (ed. Philip Harbottle and Sean Wallace, 1998) - 'Gift Wrapped'
- *Fantasy Annual 3* (ed. Philip Harbottle and Sean Wallace, 1999) - 'Fallen Angel'
- *Gryphon Science Fiction and Fantasy Reader 1* (ed. Philip Harbottle, 1999) - 'Talk Not at All'
- *Fantasy Annual 4* (ed. Philip Harbottle and Sean Wallace, 2000) - 'Afternoon'
- *Fantasy Quarterly 1* (ed. Philip Harbottle, 2001) - 'The Inevitable Conflict'
- *Fantasy Adventures 1* (ed. Philip Harbottle, 2002) - 'Child of Earth'
- *Fantasy Adventures 2* (ed. Philip Harbottle, 2002) - 'Figona', 'Emergency Exit'
- *Fantasy Annual 5* (ed. Philip Harbottle and Sean Wallace, 2003) - 'Lazarus'
- *Fantasy Adventures 3* (ed. Philip Harbottle, 2003) - 'Illusion'
- *Fantasy Adventures 4* (ed. Philip Harbottle, 2003) - 'The Greater Ideal'

- *Fantasy Adventures 5* (ed. Philip Harbottle, 2003) - 'The Answer'
- *Fantasy Adventures 6* (ed. Philip Harbottle, 2003) - 'Food for Friendship'
- *Fantasy Adventures 7* (ed. Philip Harbottle, 2003) - 'Sell Me a Dream'
- *Mammoth Book of New Terror* (ed. Stephen Jones, 2004) - 'Mirror of the Night'
- *Fantasy Adventures 8* (ed. Philip Harbottle, 2004) - 'Jackpot'
- *Fantasy Adventures 9* (ed. Philip Harbottle, 2004) - 'Spawn of Jupiter'
- *Fantasy Adventures 10* (ed. Philip Harbottle, 2004) - 'The Dilettantes'
- *Fantasy Adventures 11* (ed. Philip Harbottle, 2004) - 'Agent'
- *Fantasy Adventures 12* (ed. Philip Harbottle, 2006) - 'You Go'
- *Space:1999 - Shepherd Moon* (ed. Mateo Latosa, 2010) - 'Dead End'

To Peter, Jean, Martin and Julie Dixon

foreword

Following the death of E.C. Tubb in 2010, in my capacity as literary agent for his estate, I was approached by a leading UK publisher who made me an offer I couldn't refuse for digital rights to ALL of Tubb's more than 100 science fiction novels. But the author's "franchise" TV-tie in "Space 1999" novels were not part of the deal.

On "Space 1999", whilst Tubb owned the copyright in his novels, a publisher would have to *separately negotiate a deal with the successors to Associated Television to purchase their agreement to use the books.* This was perfectly do-able, of course, but since they already had over 100 titles my publisher decided they wouldn't bother with this added complication ...so passed them up.

But, whilst most of the Tubb Space 1999 books were based on actual TV scripts, *two of them were not:* ALIEN SEED and ROGUE PLANET were *entirely original* Tubb storylines—he just used the TV characters in his *own* storylines (making them much superior, in my view, to the other books!).

Shortly before he died, I worked with Tubb to revise the first of these, ALIEN SEED, changing the names of all the characters (most of which were his own characters anyway—only the "leads" were the TV characters)—and take out the "runaway moon" background. ALIEN SEED was set entirely on the moon itself, so this was easy to do: Tubb simply changed it to a "moon base" on a normal stable moon. The revised novel was entitled CHILD OF SPACE.

After it was completed, Tubb had worries and doubts about its viability for UK or US (English market) on the lines of "Some readers will recognize its origin and kick up a fuss with the publisher. I don't want that hassle!" He was quite ill at the time, so I respected the decision (though I disagreed with it), and the "new" novel remained unpublished, stored digitally in my pc.

In 2015 I was approached by Endeavour Press, a new UK digital and POD publisher who were interested in publishing any available books by Tubb. I promptly edited a number of new collections of sf short stories for them, which they were happy to publish, but I explained to them that only his "Space 1999" novels were currently free. I invited them to get a licence from ATV's successors for the "original" Space 1999 books—but, suspecting that they too might pass on this added complication, I also revealed that I had a digital file of CHILD OF SPACE. If they'd like to consider publishing this book (entirely Tubb's own property) I'd be happy to send the digital file for THEIR consideration. And I myself would undertake to revise ROGUE PLANET for them, to take out all the TV trappings. Endeavour predictably passed on the Space 1999 titles but commissioned me to provide the two "new" books for them; ROGUE PLANET became DESTROYER OF WORLDS. Both books were duly published in paperback and Ebook.

But then enter Mateo Latosa and Powys Media in July 2019. Mateo told me: "I am writing to you because, with the release of Year One, we would like to see if it is possible to license Rogue Planet for publication as part of the Space: 1999 series of novels. We have republished John Rankine's Android Planet and Phoenix of Megaron, but Rogue Planet by E. C. Tubb is the one title that has not seen print since the 1970s."

To which I replied: "As regards Rogue Planet, I certainly have no objection in principle to its republication by you. However, there is a problem, of which you seem to be unaware, because you make no mention of it." I then explained how, because English publishers were reluctant to reprint this novel and others because of its TV franchise, Tubb's two original novels were currently in print as CHILD OF SPACE and DESTROYER OF WORLDS. To now publish the original version of the latter as ROGUE PLANET would be a breach of Endeavour's copyright and would create confusion amongst readers buying both books—only to discover they were the same story. So I had to turn down his request.

Mateo was very disappointed at this rebuff. He explained that when he had first approached me for the rights to publish the Space: 1999 First Year novelizations, he'd had no idea where the original novels would fit in the overarching continuity he was barely beginning to put together. Just the novelizations (of Years One and Two) meant twelve entire books added to Powys's own original novels. That had been primarily the reason he didn't pursue Rogue Planet at the time. Wasn't there *some* way that Powys might be allowed to add Rogue Planet to their canon—bringing it back into the fold, so to speak? He had already edited the novel (name changes, small continuity references to past events, etc., to fit the "Powysverse" continuity and universe of characters.

After chewing things over, I wrote to James Faktor, Publishing Director at Endeavour Media, and shared my correspondence with Mateo. I pointed out that since the contract was made the original Endeavour Press had rebranded as Endeavour Media, whose business model was not to publish any more POD editions, but to concentrate entirely on Ebook editions. However, their old POD editions remained in force. Powys were publishing paper editions only, NOT Ebooks. Accordingly, if Endeavour simply surrendered their POD paper print rights to me, I would then be free to conclude my own new agreement with Powys for ROGUE PLANET—paper editions only—not Ebooks. Endeavour's Ebook edition of DESTROYER OF WORLDS would not be affected and would continue unchanged.

To my great delight, James very kindly agreed, and so at long last, fans of Space 1999 can now read Tubb's original novel!

SPACE: 1999
ROGUE PLANET

one

There were times when John Koenig wished that more than Earth had been left behind when, on that black day in September 1999, the Moon had blasted free from its age-old orbit to begin its fantastic journey through the universe. There were irritations and annoyances he could have done without and, at the moment, Sarah Pulcher was the worst.

"Commander!" she gushed. "I need you. We all need you. Please?"

"No."

"But if you would only reconsider. You would be ideal for the part."

"No," snapped Koenig again, then softened the harshness of his tone a little. Sarah Pulcher wasn't really bad, she was just a dedicated idealist determined to get her own way, a trait he could appreciate. "You don't need me, Sarah. From what I hear you've a superb company and I'm sure you'll put on a magnificent performance."

If not, it wouldn't be because of failure on her part but, looking at the dark intensity of Koenig's face—the sweep of black hair, the eyes, the sensitivity of the mouth, the firmness of the jaw—it was hard not to feel regret. H e would have made a perfect H amlet. Tall, a little too old for accurate representation, perhaps, but his added maturity would have given a greater depth to the role. A nd, too, the presence of the Commander would have guaranteed success.

Watching her, guessing her thoughts, Koenig inwardly smiled. O dd talents had appeared among the personnel of Moonbase A lpha once they had been irrevocably divorced from their home world. When the Moon left orbit, Ken L ucas, an artist by trade and soul, had been assigned to reinvigorate the romanticism of space ex ploration, but he now was remembered as one of their fallen brethren. Now, new artists appeared among them —sculptors, musicians, actors—but who would have guessed that the short, dumpy woman now standing before him would have blossomed into a producer of Shakespearian plays? From the treas-ured books and folios in her room it was obvious that she was a dedicated follower of the Bard and was now, in a sense, achieving a lifelong ambition.

"Commander?" She had been studying his face, catching the slight, almost imperceptible movement of muscle and tissue, reading the interplay of intent and emotion. "You don't object?"

"To the play? O f course not."

"I was thinking of my req uest, Commander. H ave you decided?"

ROGUE PLANET

That was another matter. Sarah Pulcher was a materials engineer and as such of more value to the base than any producer of plays. Yet men could not live on bread alone. They had to be given periods of recreation and the opportunity to relax . The theatre was a new project and could provide the essential ingredient of actual participation which recordings, no matter how good, could not. A ctors and audience, interchanging roles, maintaining a dialogue, building the family-like affinity the A lphans must have if they hoped to survive.

A nd, to be happy and content, it was essential to ensure job satisfaction. The woman would do her job as before should he insist but, subconsciously, she would be resentful and prone to error.

Koenig said, "You're important to us in more ways than one, Sarah. A lpha can't afford to lose your skills. If—"

"My assistant is perfectly capable of conducting the routine, Commander," she said q uickly. "A nd I will always be available. I promise that you will have no reason to regret granting my re-q uest." A nd then she added, with almost frightening intensity, "Please, Commander. Please!"

A cruel man or a sadistic one would have kept her on a hook, but Koenig was neither. A stupid one would have rejected her application, blind to the long-term advantages, but no fool would ever have gained the command of Moonbase A lpha, and no stupid man could ever have held that command once they had plunged deep into the unknown.

Sitting back in his chair Koenig smiled. "It's yours, Sarah. A s from this moment you are officially head of the theatre company. But I warn you, you'll have to be good or someone will be after your job."

"If I'm not good they will have the right to take it." She returned his smile, a woman glowing with happiness. "A re you positive you won't take a part, Commander?"

"No."

"Not even a small one? I could arrange— "

"If you keep tormenting me, I'll have you put in chains!" H is scowl accentuated the mock anger of his voice, a display which confirmed her belief in his acting abilities. "Now move!"

"Yes, my lord. A t once, my lord." She made a curtsey, as mocking as his feigned rage, a gesture which seemed to bring with it the rustle of billowing skirts, the dance of candlelight, the grace of a departed age. "U ntil the first night then, my lord. I shall see that you get one of the best seats."

H e rose as she left, stretching, feeling pleasure at happiness given, warmed by the woman's radiated joy. A iming his commlock, he opened the wide doors and stepped into the ordered activity of Main Mission.

A s always, he looked at the Big Screen.

It showed the space lying ahead, the area into which the Moon was relentlessly moving. A great emptiness dotted with the gleam of a multitude of stars, glowing points of distant brilliance, the sheets and curtains of haz y luminescence, the blurred fuz z of remote nebulae. A n awe-inspiring spectacle which always gripped him and made him conscious of the relative insignificance of mankind. Tiny creatures living on a mote of dust lost in the tremendous vastness of the universe. Even on their own planet they had been minute. Now, adrift on what had been their satellite, they were poised on the very edge of ex tinction.

But they had minds and intelligence and the will to survive.

They were human and they were of Earth.

"Nothing, Commander." Sandra Benes reported from where she sat at her instruments, answering the q uestion in his eyes as he looked at her. "Space registers empty as far as we can scan."

"Kano?"

"Computer verifies." H e touched the bulk of his charge. "A ll ex trapolations show an absence of any form of potential danger."

"G ood." Koenig felt himself relax even more. It would be good simply to concentrate on the inner workings of A lpha, to plot new lines of activity, to forge ahead with ex pansion and construction. A nd all without the need of strain or urgency. The play had come at a good time.

Paul Morrow mentioned it from where he sat at the main console.

"D id you decide about Sarah Pulcher, Commander?"

"Yes."

"A nd?"

"I've given her the go-ahead. There seemed no harm in it, and she's earned the chance."

"She's certainly worked on that play of hers," said Paul. "Every spare moment she's had she's been working on costumes and make-up and all the rest of it. R ight, Sandra?"

"That is right, Paul."

"I said she should try for a part. She would make a fine D esdemona, right, D avid?"

Kano smiled with a display of teeth startlingly white against the rich brownness of his skin. "That's right," he agreed. "A nd I'd make a good O thello."

"The best. A nd you, Commander? What part do you fancy?"

The part of Moses, of bringing his people home safe from the wilderness, but Koenig didn't say so.

From where he lay on the bed G reg Sanderson could see the edge of the desk, the rounded curve of a shoulder and a glint of blonde hair. A careless nurse had left the door of the ward open and so provided him with a view, but, intriguing as it was, he would willingly have changed it for another, far more bleak, perhaps, but also far more familiar.

"G reg?" Tony Ellman, occupying a bed opposite, lifted his head from the pillow. "Can you see if she's moving?"

"She isn't."

"When she does, wave at her. A ttract herattention in some way. I want to get out of here."

"Who doesn't?" Sanderson moved, cursing his leg, the inattention which had sent him toppling into a shallow crevasse to land awkwardly, to send him to Medical with a broken shin. "They've fitted Stadlers," he said bitterly. "The bone's reinforced with metal plates and still they keep me cooped up in bed like a sick child. D octor!"

A t the desk the woman stirred.

"D octor R ussell!" yelled Sanderson again. "H ere, please!"

H elena lifted her head and sat for a moent deciding whether or not to answer the call. The patient was in no danger and she could guess what he wanted.

"D octor!"

Sighing, H elena R ussell moved a heap of papers to one side and rose. A nurse could have answered the call and would have done so had she summoned one, but the nurse on duty was probably engrossed and the others would be eq ually engaged. A nd, as she had cause to remember, G reg Sanderson had an overpowering manner. It took ex perience to be able to handle an aggressive male patient and the conflict would provide a welcome distraction from the statistics she had been studying.

"D octor R ussell!" Sanderson smiled at her as she entered the ward. Big, strong, muscles toughened by long and arduous labor, he bulked huge beneath the covers. The hood lifting the sheet off the injured leg gave him a lopsided appearance. With an easy movement he lifted himself to sit upright in the bed. "D octor, when do I get out of here?"

"A nd me, D octor." Tony Ellman, smaller but just as pugnacious in his way, didn't intend to be ignored. "I've work to do and it won't get done with me lying here. H ow's about it?"

"I've one answer for the pair of you," she said flatly. "No."

"No?" Sanderson frowned. "No, what?"

"No, you can't get up, you can't get out, you can't return to duty." H elena lifted the board from the foot of the bed. "Now listen to this, G reg Sanderson. You were brought in here from outside suffering from a broken shin, multiple contusions, slight narcosis and shock. In fact, you are lucky to be alive. I intend to keep you that way given a little help."

"I feel fine."

"O f course. You've been drugged to eliminate pain. You've had a long rest under electro-sleep. G lucose and saline have been fed into your veins. The broken bone has been treated and, when the wound heals, you'll be as good as new. But not yet."

"Why not, D octor?" H e scowled. "L ook, I feel just fine and I should know. I can get up this very moment. D amn it, D octor, why the hell do I have to stay here in bed like some broken-down cripple?"

Helena said coldly, "What is your job, Sanderson?"

"What?" Her sudden chill had startled him. "I'm a surface technician. I work outside mostly, exploring the surface, checking for fissures and maintaining the scanners. Why?"

"Do I try to teach you your job?"

"No, but—"

"Then don't try to teach me mine. If you want to get up, then go ahead. Your leg might take what you intend to give it, but on the other hand, it might not. The wound could become infected and that could lead to amputation." Helena glanced at the board. "I see you're fond of wrestling—lose a leg and you might have to find another hobby. But that's up to you. If you want to take the chance, go ahead." Her tone chilled even more. "But remember this—discharge yourself and you're on your own. Don't come whining back to me for help if things go wrong. Well?"

She was bluffing; never would she permit any patient to leave unless he was a hundred percent fit, and certainly she would never withhold medical aid to any who might need it, but Sanderson didn't know that and couldn't afford to take the chance. He lay silent for a moment, thinking, remembering how dependent he and every other Alphan was on the sole source of medical assistance, the skill and dedication of the woman and her staff. And she had been right—as a technician he could appreciate that. Each to his own specialty.

"Well?" Ellman watched from across the room. "What's it to be, G reg?"

"You wanted out too."

"I know," admitted the other man. "Now I'm not so certain. H ow much longer will it be, D octor?"

"For you another three days. For you," she looked at Sanderson, "a day ex tra. I want to make sure those sutures have taken. If there is any infection, I want to catch it at once and, to be frank, I can't trust you to take things easy." Warmth edged into her voice, a calculated intimacy to remove the sting from the metaphorical slap she had given. "You big men are always so difficult. A t times I think you've never really grown up." Then casually she added, "H ow close are you to becoming wrestling champion?"

The q uestion pleased him, removing the last of any irritation he might have felt, soothing any bruise to his pride.

"Close," he said with a touch of pride. "Crato's in the lead, but I can wipe out his advantage as soon as I can put serious weight back on this leg. You should come and see me at work, D octor. A s a student of anatomy, you might be interested."

"In what?" snapped Ellman. "In *you*, you big ape? The lady has more to do than inflate your ego. A nyway, you're inefficient, right, D octor? H muscles burn too much ox ygen and his bulk takes too much energy to move around. Yes?"

"That's a matter of opinion."

ROGUE PLANET

"No, it isn't." H e was q uick to the attack. "I've read about it and Shermeen Williams verified it. She works in the hydroponic farms and she's a dietician. She told me all about the relative efficiency of fuel intake to energy output and big, bulky men have a less efficient metabolism than, well, someone like me, for ex ample."

"R ubbish! A nd isn't she too young for you?"

Ellman was taken aback, "What the—I never!" Then, realiz ing Sanderson's effort at diversion, he said, "A nd no, it isn't!" H e appealed to H elena. "A ren't I right, D octor? Tell that big ape I'm right."

"No," she said. "Fight it out between yourselves—but the first one who moves an inch from his bed gets immobiliz ed for a week. I mean that!"

A threat which would prevent any actual physical violence and restrain them to verbal battle. A t least, for them, it would pass the time and ease boredom.

H elena leaned her back against the closed door and closed her eyes. A lways she had the nagging fear of the unknown and Sanderson's leg was a problem. The wound hadn't acted as it should, which was the real reason she had kept him in bed. Stadlers, correctly applied, mended the bone and allowed immediate movement of the affected limb. But while the surgery had been without fault, the healing process was unaccountably slow.

A n unsuspected result of prolonged ex posure to the wild radiations of space, perhaps? A n effect of working in the harsh and unfamiliar environment outside? O nset diabetes? Even the low gravity coupled with alien physical demands could have been a contributing factor.

There was so much they didn't understand.

"D octor?" Mathias was walking towards her. Smiling, he nodded at the closed door of the ward. "Trouble?"

"A n argument, that's all."

"Serious?"

"No." She took a deep breath and returned his smile. "Just boredom, Bob, but I've taken care of it. Was there something?"

"Yes," he said. "It's time you were getting ready to attend the play."

Koenig called for her, waiting as she fastened the flower he had brought to the shoulder of her uniform, a lovely thing, one of delicate color and form, bright with golden flecks against a background of smoldering scarlet.

"A n orchid," he said. "A t least I think it is. There are so many kinds you can never be sure."

"Thank you, John." She rested her hand on his arm, aware of the fine lines of strain marking his face, the added tension creasing the flesh at the corners of his eyes. A n older face than he had worn when first taking over the command of A l-pha, one which had seen more than its share of death and danger, of the pit which waited, ever hungry, at the edge of the tiny world which they called their own.

"I would have brought you chocolates," he said, "but they'd just sold the last box ."

"Just as well," she said, entering into the spirit of the fantasy. "A nd I should have changed out of this dreadful uniform. Well, Commander, are we ready?"

With a flourish he ex tended his arm. "Yes, my lady, let us now go to witness the trials and tribulations of a most unhappy prince of D enmark."

A nd to witness just what Sarah Pulcher had managed to accomplish.

A s far as Koenig could see, the woman couldn't be faulted. A s he guided H elena to her seat in the auditorium, he studied the ceiling and walls. Patrick O sgood and his crew continued to transform the sterile world into a tribute to human resilience. The place had been gouged from the L unar rock, the stone smoothed and polished, panels set up together with lights and decorations so that the area was reminiscent of the great theaters of Europe. Naturally there were differences—no R oyal Box for one and no serried tiers, no orchestra pit either and no heavy proscenium—but the general atmosphere had been captured and held. H ere was a place in which make believe would find a home. A shrine dedicated to the art of mime and gesture, of words and song, of graceful shapes and monsters moving through the intricacies of an artificial world.

H abit made Koenig reach for his commlock.

"Paul?"

Morrow's face looked from the tiny screen. H e, along with others, remained on duty, a skeleton staff which maintained observation. "Commander?"

"A ll well?"

"Everything is under control," Morrow assured. "Space is as empty as far as we can scan. A ll systems functioning on optimum level. D on't worry, Commander. R elax and enjoy yourself."

A nd don't keep bothering me, thought Koenig, adding the unspoken comment. U nfairly, perhaps, but he could guess how the other felt and knew that he had made a mistake in making the check. U nless subordinates were shown they were trusted, they would become unfit for trust.

"John?" H elena smiled at him as he took his place at her side. "Trouble?"

"No, just making a routine check. H ow is your section?"

"Bob can handle it," she said firmly. "This is the first play I've had the chance to see since we left Earth and I'm not going to spoil it. Now relax , John, and forget duty for a while."

Something he could never do, but for a few hours at least he could push it deep into the back of his mind. A nd the atmosphere of the theatre helped. A t the chime of a bell the lights began to lower and a blur of light and shadow drifted across the curtain. Music filled the air, soft, the throb and pulse of tambours and sackbuts, of flutes and horns. Music which augmented the illusion of being carried back in time to another world, another place.

The curtains opened and they looked at Elsinore.

It was magic, thought Koenig. The art of the illusionist, scenes created from light and shadow, props, plaster, paint and suggestion. Bergman had helped and would even now be behind the scenes busy with his electronic wiz ardry, but the setting, the atmosphere, the choice of the men and women who now appeared in costume—all were a tribute to the skill and dedication of Sarah Pulcher, who had taken words and directions and made them come alive and real.

The genius of William Shakespeare presented by the most unusual travelling company of players ever.

With a contented sigh, Koenig relax ed and sank into the illusory and famous world of the Bard.

There had, he knew, been better productions of the play, but he doubted if any had been more eagerly received by an audience which surely was the most receptive there could be. The actors too, a little rough, perhaps, but gaining confidence as the minutes passed, their roughness adding to rather than detracting from their roles. Francisco, Bernardo, H oratio and Marcellus. The King was a giant, his Q ueen a mature accompaniment, H amlet himself a tall figure of incipient madness, flashes of paranoia merged with the bitter necessity of acceptance, the frustration of thwarted desire.

"Clever," whispered H elena at his side. "Sarah was shrewd to illuminate the incestuous desire of the son for the mother and to be able to bring it across so soon."

"H amlet for G ertrude? The O edipus Complex

"Yes. It's obvious when you have the clue and Sarah's managed to leave it in no doubt. R emember H amlet hates his uncle but as yet has no knowledge of his guilt as a murderer. The hate, as such, is illogical unless we accept the strong sex - ual motivation which drives it. O nce that is accepted all the rest falls into place. The revelations of the ghost simply provide an ex cuse and justification for revenge." H er hand closed tightly on his arm. "H ush now. H ere it comes."

The curtains parted for Scene V and the prince's communication with the ghost of his murdered father. Mist trailed across the platform, dimming the appearance of detail, the distant figures, barely observed, of waiting attendants. H amlet was in the foreground, a cunningly aimed spotlight illuminating his features with a pale, nacreous glow, not too dim to take the attention from the disturbingly frightening appearance of the apparition he faced.

Somewhere in Koenig's brain a connection was made and, suddenly, he was a boy again, sitting in a classroom, mouthing words by rote, taking the part of the ghost.

ROGUE PLANET

I am thy father's spirit;
D oomed for a certain term to walk the night,
A nd for the day confin'd to fast in fires,
Till the foul crimes done in my days of nature
A re burnt and purged away. But that I am for-
bid
To tell the secrets of my prison-house,
I could a tale unfold....

A spirit condemned to eternal suffering for the sake of sins unshriven, a relic of a time when men believed in the punishment which waited after death to sear and corrode all who had not kept the faith.

Koenig blinked, narrowing his eyes as he watched the ghost. Bergman's magic was superb. The thing seemed almost transparent, the gleam of a subdued torch showing through the rotting shroud. The voice itself, booming, sepulchral, grated on ears and nerves and sent little chills running up his spine. A voice augmented by the use of subsonics, he guessed, bolstered by a se-lection of vibratory freq uencies designd to acti-vate the fear-centers of the brain.

Turning he whispered, "H elena-"

"H ush!" H er tone was savage. "L isten, John. L isten!"

The ghost again.

O H amlet! what a fallinoff was there;
From me, whose love was of that dignity
That it went hand in hand even with the vow

made to her in marriage; and to decline
U pon a wretch whose natural gifts were poor
To those of mine!

H elena was entranced as were all in the auditorium. G lancing around Koenig could see the rapt faces and unwinking eyes, feeling the strained tension as if it were a tangible thing, almost tasting the sheer concentration directed at the stage. They were enamored, entrapped, caught in the illusion of the play.

Sarah Pulcher could have received no better reward.

From the stage the eerie voice continued, lifting, throbbing, demanding full attention. A grim voice, chill in its condemnation, ruthlessly twisting a nature already warped. The hand of the dead reaching out to ruin the lives of those left behind.

Thus was I, sleeping, by a brother's hand,
O f life, of crown, of q ueen, at once dispatched,
Cut off even in the blossoms of my sin,
U nhousel'd, disappointed, unanel'd,
No reckoning made, but sent to my account
With all my imperfections on my head;
O , horrible! O , horrible!
Move not ahead on this thy present path to ru-
in,
But retreat! Withdraw! R eturn!
Yield unto the necessity of the time,
G o! L eave! Move not into peril!
Turn back! Back! Back!

ROGUE PLANET

Words never written by the Bard and which never should have been uttered in such a contex t. Koenig felt H elena stiffen at his side, heard the sudden hum from the audience. Some, a very few unfamiliar with the play, had spotted nothing amiss. O thers had.

"Those words!" H elena looked at Koenig. "They don't belong. John, what is V ictor playing at?"

"Maybe the ghost got out of hand?" Koenig glanced at the stage. "L ook! It's changing!"

The scabrous image of rotting shroud and leprous flesh dissolved into something tall and regal. O ne arm lifted and the face, wreathed by a full, white beard, tilted, illuminated by an inward light.

"H alt! Take warning! You are about to enter a region of space containing ex treme danger. R e-treat while you are able. Nothing but fear and destruction lie ahead. You will know only devastation and death. R etreat! R eturn! Withdraw! You have been warned!"

The figure swelled, dissolving, emitting a wave of almost tangible dread, an emotion which caused men to cry out and women to scream as they cowered in their seats hiding their eyes, their ears.

V ictims of the panic which ruled the entire base.

t w

Professor V ictor Bergman was an old man with a high forehead and a mechanical heart which had given him life and, so some hinted, had robbed him of all human emotion. A lie, as Koenig well knew. The device had ex tended a valuabl life and had given an already clear brain an even greater clarity; but intelligent as that brain was, it found itself baffled.

"I don't understand it, John. A ll the scanners report only negative results. There was certainly no massive electromagnetic energy field which affected our life-support systems. If the evidence wasn't against it, I'd say that it was the result of a simple mass hysteria caused by a careless use of sonic stimulators, the kind Balor once used against us."

"A nd it isn't?"

"No, John." Bergman shook his head to em-phasiz e the point. "I've checked, no such signal was broadcast through the communications net. A nd as for the system employed in the theatre, its range was strictly limited. In any case the projec-tion would never have been able to penetrate the rock surrounding the auditorium and, as we know, the panic was one which encompassed the base."

"H elena?"

"It was a feeling, John," she reported. "A wave of sudden, inex plicable terror which momentarily disorganiz ed the entire personnel of A lpha. A ll agree on certain points; the desire to run, to hide, to withdraw. Fortunately, it didn't last long enough to endanger anyone."

"No visual stimuli?"

For a moment she hesitated, then said, "Not that anyone will admit to. A s far as it goes, those in the auditorium are the only ones who actually saw anything unusual. A nd not everyone will ad-mit to that now."

A selfprotective refusal to accept the evidence of their own senses and a natural one. H allucina-tions were always worrisome, and no one would be willing to admit they suffered from them. A nd yet Koenig had no doubt as to what he had seen and heard. Neither had H elena but Bergman, odd-ly, had less certainty.

"I was in the projection booth," he ex plained. "A s you know the ghost was a hologram projeted on a cloud of controlled vapor. We used a gas with a high metallic content and managed to shape and move it by the use of powerful mag-netic fields. R ather effective, do you agree?"

"Wonderful," said Koenig, dryly. "But the voice?"

"Projected through electronic filters. The sonic emitters were set facing the auditorium, of course. The strength of projection was two degrees above the lower level of conscious awareness. A n application of subliminal influence, you understand." H e broke off, coughing, suddenly aware that he had been rambling. "I'm sorry to be a poor witness, John, but if we caused what happened then I am totally unaware of how it was done. The energies involved simply don't lend themselves to such a conclusion."

"What you are saying is that what happened could not have been caused by any actions of our own. Is that it?"

Bergman drew in his breath. "Yes, John. That is what I'm saying."

"H elena?"

"I've checked V ictor's figures as far as I'm able and I must agree with him," she said. "Certainly, the sonic projectors could never have affected the entire base, and we do know that all personnel ex perienced the sudden emotional panic, though in a greater or lesser degree. The node seems to have been the auditorium. It was also the point of greatest visual derangement. A t least more people were willing to admit they saw something there than anywhere else."

"A nd the words?" Koenig stared from one to the other as neither made comment. "I take it that we did hear the words?"

"We did, John, yes," admitted H elena.

"We? You mean you and I? H ow about the others? V ictor?"

ROGUE PLANET

Koenig frowned as Bergman shook his head. They had met in his office, the wide doors leading to Main Mission now closed. R ising from behind his desk he crossed the floor with short, impatient strides. The lines of his face were deep, the contours set in rigid planes.

H e said curtly, "There's a mystery here and I want to solve it. A fictional ghost turns into a bearded prophet and—"

"Bearded?" H elena looked startled. "John, that figure didn't have a beard. It was clean-shaven and wore a dress suit with a decoration of some kind."

"It was bearded," said Koenig. "A t least the thing I saw had a beard and a robe of some kind. You say it wasn't—which means?"

"If the both of you looked at the same thing and each saw a different image then there is only one thing it can mean." Bergman was positive. "What you saw was subjective, not objective. In other words, it wasn't really there, you only imagined it was."

"H elena?"

"I agree with V ictor. It is the only way to ex - plain the differing reports I've received. Even accounting for hysteria and natural diversity in recounting a traumatic ex perience, there is too much divergence. Some are too vague to be even logical; others mention octopoidal and polypoidal creatures as if they were recounting the stuff of nightmare. Nonsense, of course, but illuminating."

ROGUE PLANET

"Nightmare," said Koenig. H e looked at his left hand, the fingers were clenched and, deliberately, he forced himself to spread them, flex ing them, easing the tension, masking the fear they had betrayed. "We each saw something, a creature of authority or nightmare which could, psychologically, mean the same thing. Most of us, in our time, have been scared by authority, so it is merely a transference of symbols. Never mind that for the moment. L et's take a look at what we have. Something, some ex ternal force, caused a form of mass hallucination. R ight?"

"U ntil we have a better ex planation, John, that will serve as a working hypothesis," said Bergman. "H elena?"

"I agree."

"The nex t q uestion," said Koenig, grimly, "is just what the hell caused it. A nd how?"

"What, I don't know," said H elena. "But I can take a guess as to how. I think it was done, or caused, by direct stimulation of the brain. Normally, we see something and the image is carried via the optic nerve to the brain where it is resolved into a recogniz able shape and subject. Now, if we stimulate the correct centers of the brain the reverse can happen. A subject can be made to see something which isn't actually there. The same applies to hearing, of course. In fact, I can produce ex actly those results in my laboratory."

"By hypnotism?" Bergman was interested.

"That is one method, but I was thinking of electrical cortical stimulation with the use of probes."

"Hypnotism," said Koenig. R eturning to the desk he leaned on it, resting the flats of both hands on the surface. "We were entranced, enamored, concentrating on the play. Everyone was. The ghost was a shifting, flickering image, ex actly what would lead to a hypnotic trance condition. A m I making sense?"

"Yes and no," said H elena. "O ur concentration would have made us vulnerable to group suggestion and eq ually so to response to cortical stimulation, but we can rule out simple hypnotism. There would have had to be a director or directive of some kind. A prompter to tell us what to see. A nd you are forgetting the words."

The warning. Koenig straightened and glanced towards the closed doors. Beyond them, he knew, sensitive instruments were sending their findings to digital readouts, to dials, to shifting graphs, all to be studied and correlated by skilled personnel and the mammoth abilities of the computer. Yet despite all their skill and technology, they had found nothing.

"H alt," he said thickly. "R etreat. Withdraw R eturn. D eath and devastation lie ahead. D id you all get it?"

"In one form or another, yes." H elena touched the fullness of her lower lip with the tip of her tongue, as if even thinking of the episode had dried the natural saliva. "It could be a natural accompaniment to the hallucination. We are all afraid of what could lie ahead and we would all like to return, to go back, to be safe."

A n answer, but not a good one. The mystery remained and with it the fear and anx iety. Koenig didn't believe in natural happenings. For each event there had to be a reason, and to find ex pla- nations in the realm of philosophical abstractions was to dodge the issue. A t times such dodging was of no importance. O n Earth, for ex ample, odd accounts of strange sightings and inex plicable events had been dismissed or ignored without apparent detriment. But they were not on Earth. They had little or no reserves. A mistake, any mis- take, could be the last they would make.

O n the Moon there was simply no room for the unknown.

"V ictor, run that projection again and repeat the seq uence up and down forward and back with varying strengths of sonic projection. A sk for vol- unteers. I want to check there was no possibility that the occurrence wasn't of our own doing."

"I've already checked, John."

"Then do it again!" Koenig made no attempt to soften his tone. "H elena, you do the same. Tests on all, together with cross-q uestioning. H ypnotic recall if you think it necessary. With enough in- formation we might come up with the true an- swer."

"We may already have it," she said bleakly. "We received a warning, remember?"

"Yes," he said harshly. "To halt. To return. To withdraw. To go back. Now tell me how the hell we can possibly obey it!"

The bottle was half-empty and G reg Sanderson scowled at it, remembering a joke he had once been told, a philosophical concept which hadn't amused him then and didn't now. A bottle half empty was just that, and calling it one-half full didn't alter the amount of the contents. Well, to hell with it. When it was all gone maybe he could get more or, at least, would be out of the ward, the bed, the whole damned prison the Medical Section had become.

L ifting the bottle, he drank, swallowing the neat alcohol it contained, surgical spirit intended to ease the pain of bedsores, to clean surface areas of skin. A product of the yeast vats which helped to provide their food and which he had stolen to use as an anodyne for boredom.

H e glowered at the lowered level and gently moved his injured leg. D ays now, and still the damned thing hadn't healed. Tony Ellman had gone, smiling, eager to get back to work, making a joke as he left to see about getting a crutch. A joke in bad taste—surely it couldn't come to that, a broken leg, a gash which was slow in healing.

Q uickly he took another dink.

The nurse, damn her, had closed the door so that he couldn't see out of the ward and so was left in a form of solitary confinement foreign to his nature. H e had always liked company, the boisterous comradeship of his fellow workers, the challenge of martial arts. A big man, proud of his body, enjoying the euphoria of fitness, of using the fine engine of flesh and blood which was his own.

A gain, he moved his leg, wincing at the stab of pain. Throwing back the cover he ex amined it, frowning at the ugly red streaks running from the wound, the skin distended and tender. The doctors had seen it, had muttered over it, had filled him with antibiotics and other assorted junk all with no apparent success. Tomorrow, so he had heard, he was to be given a complete blood-change and after that, if necessary, immersion in an amniotic tank where new tissue would be grown to replace that which they would have to cut away.

H e wouldn't die and he wouldn't lose his leg but he would lose time and the championship would have been decided and he would still be in this or another ward fitted up with life-support mechanisms of one kind or another. Time which dragged past on leaden feet. Feet—the plural.

H e took another drink.

A nd, remembering Ellman's parting joke, yet another and then, because it wasn't worth saving the little which remained, he emptied the bottle and sank back with his head on the pillow staring at the central light the ward contained.

A bright light which seemed to flicker and swell and pulse as if with a life of its own. To change even as he watched. To alter.

ROGUE PLANET

Mathias heard him scream.

H e had been studying a tissue sample from the man's injured leg, frowning at the distortion of the cellular structure, testing a variety of agents and collating the results. The scream caught him as he was fitting a new slide and he swore as the glass shattered, a sliver cutting a finger so that blood dripped to stain the sterile instrument.

It came again as he straightened, a shriek which sounded less than human, a thing compounded of naked terror and heart-stopping fear.

"D octor!" A nurse came running towards him, her eyes enormous in the pallor of her face. "It's Sanderson. I—"

"G et help!" Mathias thrust past her, leaving a smear of blood from his cut hand on her uniform, the scarlet bright against the white sleeve. "Bring sedatives. H urry!"

H e heard the scream again as he reached the ward and opening the door he ran inside—to see the figure crawling on the floor, face and one hand uplifted, jagged shards of broken glass held like a dagger against his wrist. A dagger which slashed even as he watched to release a river of ruby, a stream of blood from severed veins which splashed on the legs of an eq uipment cart and dappled the floor with a crimson rain.

"Seven injured," reported H elena. "Five in shock, two, catatonic. A nd one in Intensive Care."

Koenig frowned, "Who?"

"G reg Sanderson. H e slashed his wrist with a broken bottle. Bob saw him do it. O f the injured two others are hospitaliz ed; one caught his hand in a drill press, another was burned. The other injuries are superficial and caused by collisions." She added unnecessarily, "Their panic caused them to run."

A nd one to run in an unex pected direction right toward the security of the grave. Koenig re-membered the man; he owed him his life. Since that time, he'd had little contact with him. H e pre-ferred to work outside, on the surface. By all re-ports, he was a fine worker. Not the type he would have taken for wanting nerve, but when true panic struck who could guarantee their reac-tions?

"Sanderson didn't strike me as a man who would attempt suicide," Koenig said.

H elena said, "I agree with you. A nd in light of what's happened, I have to believe his actions were due to ex ternal forces acting upon his mind, ex acerbated by his frustration with being con-fined—not to mention his having gotten drunk while on pain medication… " She shook her head.

"D o you think he still feels guilt over killing Preston?" he asked.

"H e's had a long time to think about it, John. A nd much of that time was spent alone out on the surface in his spacesuit."

"Still… "

"D on't misunderstand me. I don't believe that his actions were something he'd been contemplating. R ather, I think he might have been driven to them by the same primal panic that affected the others. In his case, it seiz ed on some sort of self destructive impulse. I don't yet know what the nature of it was. R ight now, he's in electrosleep, while we try to heal his body."

R emembering it was Mathias who'd found him, saved him, he said, "H ow is Bob now?"

"H e is a doctor and a good one."

"So?"

"A doctor gets used to the sight of blood, John. H e has to."

A nd Mathias*was* a good doctor—which said nothing about his potential human weakness and, doctor or not, he could have succumbed to the general panic as had the rest. Koenig drew in his breath, remembering a time of nightmare when fear had clogged his veins and he had cringed with the desire to run, to escape, to hide.

If he had been weak and worried and afraid of personal hurt would he have yielded as Sanderson had done?

O r was it that the man owned a far more intense imagination?

Q uestions, always q uestions, and still there were no answers. Bleakly he looked at the Big Screen in Main Mission, again seeing nothing but the cold burn of distant stars.

"Sandra?"

"Nothing, Commander." She knew the implication of his call. "Space, as far as all instrumentation is concerned, is totally empty ahead of us."

"Kano, as far as Computer is concerned, what are the ex trapolations?"

"None, Commander. There is insufficient data on which Computer can work."

Koenig felt the fingers of his left hand beginning to close. It was useless to blame a machine for not having the intuitive faculty of a man—but how much data did the damn thing need?

"Try again," he ordered. "Feed it all the information we have and, if nothing else, obtain an intelligent guess." A n inconsistency, no machine could be intelligent despite the claims of those who served them, but Kano might find some factor he had previously overlooked. With relief he saw Bergman enter Main Mission. "V ictor! A nything?"

"Yes, but all negative." Bergman cleared his throat. "A t least we can eliminate all thought of internal causes for the recent wave of panic. A ll eq uipment in the theatre was out of operation. I've checked all sources of electronic usage and none show any surge or loss, which means we can eliminate all packets of energy-source such as spatial vortices which could have created a high-order energy flow."

"Which could mean that nothing happened, and we have one attempted suicide and several others injured for no reason at all."

Koenig was being sarcastic and Bergman knew it. Q uietly he said, "There has to be a reason, John. A ll we've done so far is to eliminate sources of familiar energy but there are others and they may be the cause."

"Such as?"

"V ictor is thinking of the paraphysical, John," said H elena. "We know that some people possess the talent to move objects without physical contact, but as yet we have no means of discovering what type of energy they use. Telepathy, also, req uires a form of energy and that is eq ually unex plained even though we know that telepathy ex ists. The warning–"

"Warning?"

"It has to be that," she insisted. "Twice now we have known panic and the desire to run. The first time we heard, or thought we heard, an actual voice giving us instructions. Perhaps that was because of the unusual conditions in which we received the message."

A nd the effects on his people clearly showed it should not be ignored.

Koenig took a step forward and halted just behind where Morrow sat at the main console. Before him lamps flashed in endless signaling, one of the circuits which continually monitored the base and the surroundings.

"The Big Screen, Paul. Full magnification."

Koenig watched as the distant stars seemed to move aside, an optical illusion which gave the impression of hurtling at a fantastic velocity toward them in space. A nd still he saw nothing.

"Try filters."

The stars flickered and changed color as Morrow obeyed, feeding selective filters over the scanners, blocking out various bands of the electromagnetic spectrum while bolstering others.

The results were the same.

Nothing.

Space remained as empty as before.

Empty, but holding something which had warned them twice now to stay away. Something which could emit psychic energy to directly influence the brain. A power which warned of devastation and death unless they obeyed.

But they could not obey.

The Moon was on a set course. The A lphans had no practical means of maneuvering. No way they could dodge or slow, retreat or withdraw.

They could do nothing but hurtle on to whatever waited ahead.

"Commander?"

"That's enough, Paul. O rder an Eagle and crew to make ready for an investigation flight. Carter will want to take command—let him pick his own co-pilot."

"A d?"

"Put the base on Yellow A lert—and keep it on until further orders!"

t h r ee

L eaning back in the copilot's seat, Ivor Khokol indulged in a dream. H e was a chief of the Bandhaisai riding with A ttila, the Kagan of the H iung. Beneath the hooves of hi horse the Steppes rolled back to the East, while ahead, misted in rumor, lay the wealth of a decadent civiliz ation. Soon now they would reach the gates of R ome and the world would be theirs to loot, to burn, to take and use as they wished.

Even the thought of it sent the blood pounding in his veins to throb in his ears, sending adrenaline to stimulate nerve and muscle, sharpening his awareness, his aggression. The physical prelude to combat as it was a symptom of fear.

"Ivor!" From the pilot's chair A lan Carter glared at his companion. "Keep alert there!"

"I'm alert, Skipper."

"Then report on instrumentation during the past five minutes."

"A ll systems operating at optimum," said Khokol immediately. "Temperature of rear left lifting jet a little high but within tolerance. A ll clear on scanners. R adio contact at constant level. H umidity—"

"That's enough." A utomatically Carter scanned his own instrument panel, a shift of the eyes which had become second nature to the head of R econnaissance. A head, space, asrfas he could determine, was clear. A s clear as it had been when they left A lpha an hour ago.

Settling back, he thought about his co-pilot.

Ivor Khokol was a dreamer and a romantic of the O ld tradition, living in imagination the glories of the past, fighting ancient battles and adopting the mantle of the great. In that, there was no harm; only when it threatened his efficiency would there be cause to worry. H is immediate report had meant little. A ny serious fluctuation in the operation of the Eagle would have triggered an alarm, and in such a case, Carter would have acted. Yet he hadn't actually lied. H e had the facility of split-mind operation, turning a part of himself into a watchful automaton while allowing the rest of his mind to indulge in fantasies.

A trait which could be an asset in certain conditions but dangerous in others. No pilot, Carter knew, could be ex pected to maintain total concentration for long periods at a time. It was mentally and physically impossible to do that. Insidious fatigue would ruin finely balanced judgements and, unless recogniz ed, would lead to fatal error. A man who could watch for hours at a stretch, who would spring into full and complete awareness at any moment when triggered by something wrong, was a man ideal for routine patrols.

But for an investigation flight?

ROGUE PLANET

Carter had made his decision and had chosen Khokol to accompany him. How he acted now would determine his future with Reconnaissance.

He said, "Skipper, have you ever studied history? I mean really studied it?"

"Why?"

"I was thinking of Attila. Of how he managed to unite the tribes and sweep across plains to reach Eastern Europe. You know that he actually managed to reach Rome and would have taken it if they hadn't bought him off."

"So?"

"Think of it! A man, a barbarian in a sense, who managed to do the near-impossible. He could have made himself Emperor, become a Caesar, ruled the entire known world!"

"Instead of which," said Carter dryly, "he died in pain to be cremated by his followers. And after?"

"Nothing," admitted Khokol. "He was a strong man and there was no one to follow him. All he had built vanished almost at once. The affiliated tribes, the vassal Germanic peoples, all those who had become one force beneath his horsetail standard, all dissolved as snow in the sun. But if he had lived another ten years, or if he had managed to leave a strong heir, or if the tribes had managed to work together instead of letting petty feuds destroy their unity—who knows?"

"If pigs had wings, they would fly." Carter scanned the instruments and threw a switch. "Eagle One to Main Mission. Paul?"

"R eceiving." Morrow's face appeared on the screen. "A nything as yet, A lan?"

"No. We could be flying into a vacuum."

"You are."

"I was talking metaphorically. There's nothing out here but nothing."

"Which is the way we want it to be." Morrow smiled. "Maintain alignment, A lan. It's important."

"Will do."

The screen went blank as Carter broke the connection and, again, he checked his instruments. The target-star was a fraction out and he returned it to the center of the crosshairs with a deft touch on the controls. It was a big, blue-white sun and it could have planets and, if so, maybe they would pass close enough to investigate and, if any of those worlds could support life, they might find a new home.

If—always if.

Carter glanced around the command module of the Eagle, wondering, if and when they finally found somewhere to stay and O peration Ex odus was completed, what he would do. Fly, naturally, he could think of nothing else, but planetary flight would be odd after traversing the vast immensity of space, setting his course by the stars, lancing out from the Moon to check and probe and discover what there was to be discovered.

A nd every journey was a circle—each time he returned to A lpha.

There was no other place to go.

"Skipper!"

"What?"

"I—nothing." Khokol frowned at the instruments. "I thought I saw a flicker just then. O ne of the receptors registered. A t least I thought it did."

D reaming or not, he would have caught it and it was proof of his efficiency that Carter had not. For a moment he hesitated, studying the instruments, then again made contact with A lpha.

"Paul?"

"H ere." Morrow looked from the screen. "Trouble?"

"Could be. D id you spot anything?"

"Such as?"

"A n energy emission of some kind. O ne of the receptors kicked just now. No repetition as yet, which could mean an internal malfunction or a local nex us of limited ex tent."

"Nothing registered here, A lan."

"Then it could be local, but you'd better maintain constant observation and monitoring. We could be heading into what we're looking for."

Carter glared at what lay ahead. To the naked eye there was nothing, to the instruments the same, yet something was waiting there, he sensed it, felt it with every fiber of his being.

G rimly he resisted the urge to run. To turn the Eagle and head back to the Moon as fast as the ship would travel.

Ivor Khokol felt the same.

H e shifted in his chair, easing his body against the restraints, his hands reaching for the controls only to fall back as he realiz ed that to touch them would be useless. Carter had the control and would retain it unless there was a good reason why he should not. A nd a feeling, no matter how strong, was not reason enough for the Skipper to abandon his authority.

But if he were dead?

A n odd thought, and Khokol did his best to banish it. H e liked Carter and admired him and envied the man his skill and position. O ne day, with luck, he too would be a master-pilot and command a mission of his own. O ne day, again with luck, he might reach up to become the head of a Section. O ne day.

H e shivered, conscious of a sudden chill, then was suddenly gasping for breath. Blinking he stared ahead, concentrating on the stars, seeing them appear to shift and form new patterns. A house, a ship, a horse, the lineaments of a woman's face.

A smooth, firmly contoured visage with enigmatic eyes and a mouth which betrayed sensuality. H ollow cheeks and strong jaw, the hint of Slavic ancestry. The ears and blonde hair.

D octor H elena R ussell!

Smiling at him from the empty depths of space. Beckoning.

Khokol unfastened his restraints and lifted himself out of the co-pilot's chair. O pening the hatches, he left the command module and moved though the access corridor into the passenger module.

ROGUE PLANET

Carter thought little of it. H unger, a call of nature... despite the advanced waste collection system, sometimes the alternative to relieving oneself inside one's suit was more appealing. But then, a warning light flared on the panel beside him. Khokol was trying to open the Main H atch while the passenger module was still pressuriz ed.

"No!" A lan Carter reared in his chair, snarling at the jerk of forgotten restraints, freeing them with a blow as he leapt from his chair. H e lowered his visor and ran toward the passenger module. Seeing Khokol at the hatch controls, he lunged towards him. "D on't, you fool! D on't!"

Ivor Khokol's helmet was open and his eyes were glaz ed. O ne hand was thumbing the controls which would open the port—and beyond lay nothing but the airless void.

"Ivor!" Carter grabbed at his shoulder, turned the man, threw him back towards a passenger seat. "Seal up and strap down. That's an order!"

"I—no! I must go! I must!"

Madness. It showed in his face, his eyes, the tormented knotting of skin and muscles, and with the mania came a maniacal strength.

Carter was thrown back to crash against the hull, head ringing from the impact, details blurring as he sank to his knees. D az ed, almost unconscious, he saw the other man tear at the portal, the sudden flood of ruby from the alarms, a red flush which accompanied the strident clangor of the warnings.

"Ivor! The controls!"

"Too late!" The man turned, foam at his lips, blood running from bitten flesh. "Wait for me! Please wait for me!"

Then there was nothing but a roar of confusion and an overwhelming darkness.

"Eighty-nine hours, seventeen minutes and thirty seconds as from—now!" Bergman threw the time-control on the chronometer then looked up from where he sat at his desk. "That's how long it will take us to reach the same point as A lan did when he ran into trouble, assuming, of course, that the area remains stationary relative to this region of space."

"The Forbidden A rea," murmured Koenig. "What caused the trouble, V ictor? A barrier of some kind?"

"It could be that," agreed the professor. "A nd, coupled with the warnings, I think that it is. A final deterrent, the last warning before whatever lies behind the barrier is reached."

A nd what that could be was anyone's guess. R estlessly Koenig paced the room. Normally he liked to spend time in Bergman's laboratory, enjoying the touch of familiar things, seeing the rows of old books, the scrolls of proven accomplishment, the models and small items which Bergman had brought with him to the Moon back in the days when he had been a welcome visitor, an honored guest granted the facilities of Moonbase A lpha to pursue his investigations.

ROGUE PLANET

Now there was no time to pause and linger, to step metaphorically back in time to when life was a matter of following routine instead of the continual challenge it had now become.

Pausing he stood before a chart hanging on the wall. It bore a mass of curves, symbols representing stars, a yellow swath their progress. H is finger rested on the point where the Moon was at the moment, moved on to halt at a red smear. Knowing their velocity any schoolboy could have computed the time remaining before they reached it, but no one could know what lay beyond. "D id you manage to plot the ex tent of the area?"

"No." Bergman shook his head as he came to stand beside Koenig. "The only way would be to send out a series of Eagles and wait for something to happen. It would have taken too long."

A nd have been too ex pensive on men. Koenig glared at the chart, feeling the anger of frustration. A known enemy he could have faced but how to fight emptiness?

"A lan reported nothing visible as he approached the area," he said. "The monitoring verified his observations yet, as we know, something must lie in that region. What, V ictor? A field of energy of some kind? A destructive vortex A transdimensional warp?" H is left hand made a fist. "What the hell are we up against?"

Bergman said thoughtfully, "I'm not sure, John, but perhaps it is invisibility."

"What?" Koenig shook his head. "Invisible or not, substance still has mass. It has temperature.

It radiates energy. It can be spotted on instruments."

"Not if it rested in a spherical field," Bergman insisted. "A bubble of force which rotates all received energy through a half-circle of one hundred and eighty degrees. It is a mathematical concept, John, which we used to play with at university. H ow to become invisible. You can't do it by becoming transparent because any touch of dust or dirt will reveal you as it would a building made of glass. But if light could be rotated so that you saw not the object before you but the light it received from behind—"

"Then you wouldn't see it at all!" Koenig punched his right fist into his left hand. "O f course. A ll light and so all visibility would be curved in a half-circle, so that you would look around the object and not at it. The same would apply to all bands of the electro-magnetic spectrum. O ur instruments are registering the energies received from beyond the area, the stars we see are really occluded but we can't tell that, and so, for us, space ahead is empty. But how, V ictor? Magnetic fields?"

"If so, they must be of incredible density." Bergman was dubious. "It's possible, but I'm inclined to think a spatial warp of some kind could be responsible."

L ifting the commlock from his belt, Koenig snapped, "Main Mission. Kano? H ave the computer check on all stellar observations. I want special reference paid to any variation in apparent brightness or shift of position no matter how minute. Cross reference for signs of gravitational lensing. Full scan in direction ahead and for one hundred and eighty degrees to either side. Top priority. Sandra?"

H e waited until her face replaced Kano's on the tiny screen.

"Correlate all instrument readings for the past month against those presently received. I want detailed comparisons as to temperature and radiation fluctuations. In all future scans include D oppler compensations based on spectrum shift."

L ight had mass, it could be bent by gravitational or magnetic fields, but unless those fields were perfect there would be minor variations. If spotted, they could plot the ex tent of the bubble before them. L ight was similar to sound—advancing, it rose in pitch; retreating, it lowered. A shift to the red meant that a light source was retreating; towards the blue, that it was advancing towards them. A gain, they could only hope for minor alterations, but any information would be of value.

But none would solve the main q uestion.

"What's in there?" Koenig voiced his main worry. "V ictor, what are we heading into?"

"I don't know, John." Bergman was coldly precise. "O nly time will answer that. But there is another q uestion which should be asked."

"H ow can we defend ourselves?" Koenig looked at the other, his face grim. "I know, V ictor. A ny suggestions?"

H e was aching and sore but alive and all in one piece and, for that, A lan Carter was grateful. Cautiously he stretched, feeling the nag of bruises.

Watching him H elena said, "Take things easy for a while, A lan. Some heat and massage will help."

"Ivor?"

H e, too, was all in one piece and still alive, but, watching him through the transparent partition, Carter would have wished that if he had been in the same condition, the instruments registering his physical condition would have dropped to z ero. No man, while living, should adopt the appearance of a corpse. No pilot should be staring with dull eyes at the ceiling, his hands limply folded in his lap. No human should lie like a vegetable, unable to even smile.

Without turning his head Carter asked, "H ow long?"

"Since the trouble."

"When the Eagle went haywire?"

"There was nothing wrong with the Eagle, A lan. The fault was entirely human. D on't you remember?"

H e frowned, remembering only Khokol's sudden madness, his own confusion.

"Paul was monitoring," she ex plained. There was no need to lower her voice. Khokol, if he could hear, would make no response. If he did, it would be a step towards recovery, but even so she spoke in a whisper. "H e saw Khokol rise and head for the Main H atch and you trying to stop him. There was a struggle and you were thrown to one side. Ivor turned back towards the door but, naturally, Paul had the Eagle on remote control and he couldn't open it. H e tried, G od, how he tried, then suddenly he collapsed."

"A nd Paul brought us back to A lpha?"

"Yes. You seemed to be unconscious and when you arrived back here—"

"Seemed? I was out, surely."

"No, A lan." H elena met his eyes, her own direct. "You weren't unconscious, not in the way you mean. You were disoriented and on the edge of catatonia, but you weren't asleep or stunned."

H e said, attempting to be casual, "There's a difference?"

"Medically, yes, but we won't go into that now. It isn't important. I drugged you, gave you hypnotic therapy and some electro-stimulated sleep. Now it's your turn to help me. What happened out there?"

"You know what happened. Ivor went craz y and tried to step out into space. I tried to stop him and got hurt. I guess I was concussed— would that account for it? My condition, I mean."

H e was anx ious and H elena could guess why. A pilot had to be fit, otherwise he was useless. A man given to psychic breakdown had no place in an Eagle.

"O fficially, yes." H er smile eased his trepidation. "But there was more to it than that. D id you sense that the Eagle was out of control? V eering? Twisting, perhaps?"

"Yes."

It had maintained an even course at all times—his own sensory apparatus had been at fault, not the guidance systems of the machine.

"A nything else? D reams, perhaps? O dd visua effects? Sounds?"

"There was confusion and then darkness. Nothing else."

"A reyou certain?"

H e said stiffly, "You've known me long enough and well enough to know that I'm not a liar."

"A lan, I didn't call you that! But I need to know. It's important. Can you remember anything at all after Khokol hit you? I'm not asking you to be factual—we know what happened within the Eagle, but only you can tell us what happened in your mind. You mentioned confusion. Was it visual? D id you hear snatches of song, for ex ample? A voice? D id you ex perience a sudden, overwhelming desire of some kind? A nurge to do something?"

H e said dryly, "L ike opening the port? No. I had no intention of committing suicide."

"What then?"

For a moment he remained silent and she gained the impression of a man struggling with himself, of overcoming doubts and fears, of surrendering some private citadel.

"Ivor hit me and I fell," he said abruptly. "I was daz ed and almost out. The Eagle seemed to be spinning and twisting—you said it wasn't but that's how it felt to me. It grew dark but there were lights and, yes, a voice of some kind. It was like when you are half asleep and barely hear what's going on close at hand. The lights were flashes, dots in the shadows like stars and something moved against them. I was afraid, I think. No, I was afraid and yet at the same time resigned. There was nothing I could do. Then the darkness came, and it was like falling into an ebony cloud." H e added thoughtfully, "A fall which never seemed to end."

"Was it A rra?"

"No… No, this was different somehow."

"The voice—what did it say?"

"I don't know." H e shrugged at her ex pression. "I'm not playing games, D octor, I simply don't know. The words were blurred and almost as if they were foreign. I say ʻalmost' because there was a familiarity about them, but I couldn't make them out."

"The tone? O ne ofejection?"

"More of negation." Carter frowned as he thought about it. "Someone or something saying a certain thing was not to be. A m I making sense?"

Before answering, H elena crossed to her desk and activated an instrument. Carter heard a blur of words, questions and answers, and realiz ed that the present interrogation wasn't the first. H e had been q uestioned under hypnosis, taken from the Eagle, sedated, drugged, cross-ex amined. H is anger died as q uickly as it came. To each of them, his responsibility, and the burden of responsibility carried by H elena R ussell was far from light.

She said, "A lan, you were very young when your mother died. Correct?"

"Yes."

"But you remember her."

"No."

"You remember her," she said again. It was not a q uestion. "A person à receptive organism and all that happens close at hand is noted and filed within the cortex . Now, those lights, the shape and voice you saw and heard. I suggest that they could have been the reflected illumination of an ex ternal source. The shadow thatof a woman limned against them. The voice that of your mother telling you to be silent, perhaps. A common occurrence. You agree it might be possible?"

A n ancient memory dredged from his subconscious?

"G ood," she said as he nodded. "A s I suspected. It leads to the conclusion that the force responsible is one which triggers various rejective syndromes within the brain. If so, it accounts for the diversity of ex periences common during the warning periods. You were fortunate, A lan."

"Why?"

"You returned to early childhood. If Paul hadn't withdrawn the Eagle from that sector of space—"

"Back even further?" H e had anticipated her reasoning. "Back to the embryo?"

"Perhaps."

"Is that what happened to Ivor?"

"No." H elena glanced to where he lay, eyes open but unseeing. "H e isn't catatonic. Not in the true sense that he has retreated to early child-hood to escape the pressures of being an adult, and then having to retreat even further because childhood is not a happy time. H e has, in a sense, escaped, but in some different form. The fact he tried to open the port worries me. H e must have known the danger, which means he was subcon-sciously trying to kill himself."

"Kill himself? Ivor?"

"H e belongs to a culture in which the death wish is very strong."

A lan glanced at the ther, finding it impossible to believe that a man so strong and so fit should be eager to find death. But then remembered Sanderson. A nd in the Eagle, if one, then why not them both? Why had Khokol succumbed and he survived?

"If all men were alike, A lan, 'said H elena when he put the q uestion, "they wouldn't be men, they'd be robots. H ow do I know? Yet it's some-thing we've got to try and find out and find it soon." She glanced at per watch. "Within six ty seven hours to be ex act."

"Why?"

"Because that's when we will hit the bubble which almost sent you insane and wrecked Kho-kol's mind." She looked at where he lay. "A nd what happened to him could happen to us all!"

f ou

Nothing.

Koenig stared at the Big Screen and felt the tug and pull of frustration. With an effort he kept his face a blank mask, his hands unclenched. To be a commander was more than to give orders. A lways he had to present a confident aspect, always to radiate a confidence he might not feel and yet this time was harder than most.

H ow toi ght an enemy unseen? A danger unknown?

Before him the stars glittered with their usual brightness, the bright ex panse of the galax y glowing as if a rich scatter of gems lay on the somber velvet of a jeweler's cloth. It was hard to realiz e that between he and they rested something destructive. A thing which threatened A lpha itself. A n invisible killer edging closer even as he watched. A menace which had nearly caused the death of one man and had reduced another to a mindless shell.

For a moment Koenig had the impression of a crouching beast, alien, horrible, waiting with gaping jaws and venomous sting to grip, to hold, to suck intelligence and life from the hapless prey falling into its grasp.

A moment only, then the illusion was gone and, taking a deep breath, Koenig glanced at the chronometer.

"Minus fifteen seconds, Commander." Paul spoke from his chair. "Full strength?"

"Yes."

"For an indefinite period?" Morrow's voice held doubt. "The generators might not be able to take max imum load for too long."

"Full strength for five minutes. Cut for checking, then resume for fifteen. Check again, then operate at half power until we are an hour from impact."

A n hour from madness and maybe death and the time could be less if the bubble was moving towards them. Bergman doubted that it was. Koenig hoped that he was right.

"R eady to activate," said Morrow. "Three, two, one—on!"

A shimmer softened the glow of the stars, a ripple made of broken rainbows which strengthened even as he watched and settled into a sparkling, coruscating bowl which covered the base. Electronic wiz ardry devised by Bergman and built by Kirwan's technicians. Forces bent and twisted into channeled lines. Energies formed and held in powerful fields. A defense powered by the strength of the atomic engines, refined in the generators, fed through sq uat towers and terminals set about the area.

"L oss?"

"Two percent above normal, Commander."

"R eason?"

"Maladjustment, I think." Morrow grunted as he sent his hands flying over his controls. Before him a digital readout moved, figures glowing with ruby flame. "A slight imbalance, Commander. Now compensated. O perational efficiency now less than one percent below."

U nder test, the screen had withstood the fury of ex ploding nuclear devices, but what they faced was no familiar form of energy. The screen might be useless and probably was, yet it had to be incorporated into their defenses. Koenig glanced again at the chronometer. Two minutes remained of the initial period.

"Boost to absolute max imum, Paul."

"Commander?"

"D o it!" If the generators were to fail it was better to find out now rather than later. "L ift and hold."

The rainbow shimmer thickened, blanked the stars with its coruscating curtain, threw a lambent glow over the L unar terrain, the surface installations of the base. D istant scanners gave an ex ternal view, an inverted bowl dotted with scintillating flashes like tiny ex plosions, local flares of energy escaping from the confining fields.

"Strength falling," said Morrow. "D ecay accelerating. Power loss nine percent... eleven... fifteen—eighteen... Commander?"

"Maintain." A muscle twitched high on one cheek as Koenig watched the tell-tales on the console. A ny weakness had to be found and eliminated, suspect points strengthened, ex tra circuits incorporated if necessary.

"Twenty-one... two... " Morrow's voice rose and he half turned in his chair. "A q uarter down, Commander!"

"Maintain!"

H old the torrent of power as the gauges fell and the scintillating flashes grew, until they sparkled like a miniature battlefield over the glowing inverted bowl of the dome. U ntil the meters flashed red and the alarm stabbed the air with its warning snarl.

"Cut!" Koenig drew in his breath as the sound and flashing died. "R eport?"

'' Fifty percent loss of retrieved power—total loss close to seventy-three percent. R eserve accumulators depleted by a third. Insulation damage on generators two and five. Terminal corrosion on points three to twelve, seventeen to twenty-nine." Frowning Morrow added, "I don't understand this. The last regular maintenance report showed all installations at optimum level. Those generators should have stood up better than that."

"When was the last check made?" Koenig nodded at the answer. "Before the last warning. I thought so. Can anyone really be certain what they saw and did during that time?"

"Sabotage?" Morrow's voice echoed his incredulity. "That's tantamount to suicide. Who—?" H e broke off, remembering, feeling again the terrible revulsion, the urge to run, to hide, to escape. "Someone, maybe, tried to kill himself. H e rigged the generator in some way, hoping it would blow. Maybe, under ex ternal stress, it would have blown and taken the entire base with it. If we hadn't tested it as we did—Commander, you could have saved us all!"

A possibility, but the danger was now over. Koenig wondered what had made him abort the original test and push the screen so hard for so long. Instinct, perhaps, the cultivated inner sense which defied all logic and so often provided the right answer.

"H ave the engineers check the system," he ordered. "A ll defective parts to be replaced. Summon Professor Bergman to check and test the installation when the work has been completed." Koenig glanced at the chronometer. "A nd tell them to hurry—we have only twelve hours left before impact."

H elena R ussell was asleep and, in her sleep, a man came to her in a dream. H e was short, stocky with a neatly trimmed beard and a domed, balding skull. H e wore a ceremonial dress coat with a scarlet flower in his lapel and, crossing his torso from his right shoulder to the left hip, a wide ribbon blaz ed in gold and emerald. She had seen him three times before.

The last had been on the stage of the theatre.

ROGUE PLANET

The time before had been when he had given her the highest accolade of her profession short of the Nobel Priz e.

The first had been when, as a young student, she had been privileged to attend one of his lectures.

Years ago now, a time when both he and she had been much younger, but always she remembered him as he had been when handing her the award, neatly if fussily dressed in his old-fashioned dress coat, his inevitable flower and the sash which was the decoration he had won from the President of Z aire as a partial reward for saving ten million souls from the ravages of plague.

Professor Emmanual D ylan Batrun.

To her, once, the living symbol of ultimate authority.

A nd, in the dream, he came to stand before her, moving through wisps of swirling fog, his face blurred a little, his voice distant but as firm and impatient as she remembered. "In ancient times men thought of a person as consisting of three parts—the brain, the body and the soul. L ater, when we, in our arrogance, assumed that only ourselves had been graced with true knowledge, an adjustment was made. The brain became the mind, the body remained and the concept of the soul was medically disposed of. Now a person consisted only of two parts, the body and the mind, and it was natural to place them each in their neatly labelled compartments. If the mind was affected then the subject was insane. A s insanity ha no connection with reality as we have determined what it should be, then all statements and utterances of the poor, demented creature could be safely ignored. If the body fell ill then it could be repaired as a mechanic would mend a broken machine. In those enlightened days it was common for eminent surgeons to complain bitterly that, while their operations had been successful, the ungrateful patient had insisted on dying."

A calculated pause—time in which to take a sip of water, to adjust his flower, to move a little to ease incipient cramp, to allow the sycophantic laughter to fade into a respectful silence.

In her dream, H elena saw it all as she had seen it before. Turning, she looked at an endless ex panse of barren desert, sere beneath a lambent sun, the grit strewn with a stark litter of bone, fleshless skulls watching her with cavernous sockets, teeth bared in the parody of a smile.

O n the podium the archaic figure continued as before.

"... is a tedious thing. It is hard to accept the fact that we may have been wrong, and it is easy to look for simple answers to involved q uestions. A sane man becomes deranged—how convenient to say that a demon has possessed him. A man's body is not as it should be—obviously the humors are not working in true harmony. Words!" The dry voice held the crack of a whip. "R ubbish! What is a demon? What are humors? D efine! D efine before you can hope to understand!"

ROGUE PLANET

The figure blurred, wavered, mist rising to stream in wreaths and tendrils of luminous color. A rainbow swirled and, for a moment, she was conscious of an aching poignancy. So dear the departed days! So sweet the illusions of youth! So rich the future which had yet to come!

"D octor! D octor R ussell!"

Mathias was beside her, his face reflecting his concern. A s she opened her eyes, he lifted his hand from her shoulder.

"Bob?"

"You were restless," he said. "Crying out."

"A dream," she said. "I was young again and listening to Professor Batrun. In V ienna at the Institute. H e was talking of the interaction of body and mind." With a smooth motion she sat upright and clasped her hands around her lifted knees. "A great man, Bob. A great physician and a wonderful psychiatrist. I think it was he who guided me to take an interest in space medicine. Something he said—I can't remember just what, but a hint, maybe, a little verbal push."

"A psychological nudge." H e nodded, understanding. "Something similar happened to me. Coffee?"

"Please."

She watched as he went to get it, looking around at the nearly empty ward. She had rested for a moment on one of the beds, intending only to relax for a moment, to ease the tension of mind and body, and had obviously fallen asleep. She stretched, feeling the tug of her uniform, noting the blanket which lay to one side. Mathias had covered her, had looked in from time to time and, at the last, had touched her gently to reassure her, to offer what comfort his presence could provide.

She smiled as he returned with steaming cups of coffee.

"Thank you, Bob. Did you ever meet the professor?"

"No. He had retired by the time I graduated and was dead before I'd gained my doctorate."

A few years, she thought, suddenly reminded of the age differential between them. Less than a decade, but it had robbed him of the chance of meeting a genius.

She sipped her coffee, grateful for its warmth and comfort, mulling the accomplishments of the dead. Batrun had been a rebel, tearing down accepted beliefs, hurling challenges at the establishment, mocking ancient traditions. For years he had wandered in the wilderness, damned by his unorthodox experiments in mind-body function. An accident had saved him. The daughter of the president of some South American republic had survived a plane crash and wandered in the jungle until rescue. Saved, she had been insane. Taken to Batrun, she had been cured.

Then came the disaster at Zaire.

"He was lucky," said Mathias as if he had been reading her thoughts. "The chance of being in the right place at the right time."

"But he proved his theories."

"A nd again, was fortunate. The girl could have died or remained permanently insane." Mathias took a sip of coffee. "I wonder why you dreamed of him?"

A subconscious association, of course, but ex - actly what? Sitting on the bed, knees uplifted, sipping her coffee, H elena thought about it. The lecture itself was nothing, a replayed mental re- cording. It had only repeated elemental facts, now common knowledge, of the association be- tween mental and physical health, the basic unity of both and the influence of ex ternal sensory stimuli to each individual picture of reality. Touch a man with a red-hot poker after mentally con- vincing him that he is to be touched by ice, and he will not blister or suffer hurt. Conversely, once convinced that a feather is a sword, and flesh will part, wounds bleed and bones break beneath its impact.

"D efine!" Batrun had said. "D efine before you can hope to understand!"

D efine what?

The present problem?

What else had she been trying to do!

"D octor?" Mathias had seen the sudden ten- sion of her hand, the betrayed emotion. "Is some- thing wrong?"

"I'm a fool, Bob, that's what is wrong. We've been trying to find out what happened during the warnings and what happened to A lan and Ivor Khokol out there in space. We've been hoping to find a shield of some kind to protect us."

"So?"

"A wrong definition. We don't have to beat the situation, just find a way to live with it. We know, for ex ample, that some force is inducing mental derangement by some form of cortical stimulus. We can't prevent it as yet, but perhaps we can negate its effects in some way."

"With drugs?"

"If possible." She set aside the coffee. "Can you think of anything which would do?"

"We have q uite a selection," he said. "A lcohol, for ex ample, the ancient anesthetic. It is a depressant and throws the motor system all to hell if enough is taken. It confuses the reality sense and could work if the application and control could be maintained. U nfortunately, there are unpredictable side-effects which make its use undesirable. Tranq uiliz ers?"

"Numb emotional reaction, but we want more than a delayed reaction." H elena rose and inflated her lungs, her figure sharply prominent against the taut material of her uniform. "A s I see it the thing is to affect the synapses in some way. If mentally received stimuli can be prevented from conversion into physical activity, then we will have found some form of defense. A cetylcholine perhaps?"

"It could hold the answer," admitted Mathias. "We know it is an essential ingredient in the passing on of nerve impulses. We can destroy it with the enz yme cholinesterase, so if we could compound something combining a form of paralytic agent coupled with a reality distorter—no, D octor. There would be no way to predict the action of such a hell's brew."

"But we must try, Bob," said H elena. "We must try."

"Nothing." Sandra Benes looked up from her instruments. "Space ahead is still apparently clear. A ll receptors negative."

"Incredible!" Bergman narrowed his eyes, heavy lines creasing his cheeks. "I would have sworn that, so close to the impact point, some aberration would have been obvious. No trace of any stellar displacement on the comparison runs?"

"None."

"Nor temperature differentials?" Bergman grunted at her negative shake of the head. "Well, John, that leaves us with nothing but speculation and intelligent assumptions."

"Such as?"

"The warning field could either be of great depth and some distance from the actual area, or the forces which rotate the electromagnetic spectrum are of an immensely high order. In that case ..."

H e rambled on but Koenig wasn't paying full attention. Instead he moved to where the internal monitors scanned the interior of the base, running his eyes over the screens, noting small points and sensing again the unusual eeriness of what he saw. A lways, when the base was on R ed A lert, there was an unusual and intangible atmosphere.

A silence, a tension as of a coiled spring, an awareness which held something of the animal poised to strike, but now there was an added q uality.

The guards were in their places, the technicians at their posts, all security areas sealed. But now those doors had been welded shut, the passages were deserted, all non-essential personnel confined to their q uarters. O n the screens the rooms and corridors were deserted, and, to Koenig, A lpha had gained the appearance of a ghost town, an empty village, a tomb.

A bad thought and one he dismissed with an irritable shake of the head. A lpha was far from dead. It was a citadel prepared for the unknown. O nce the warning barrier had been passed what?

From his console Paul Morrow said q uietly, "Twenty-five minutes to go, Commander."

"The defenses?"

"A t optimum." Morrow glanced at the screens showing the coruscating bowl of protective energy which covered the base. "Ten percent more available power for emergency boost if req uired."

"Save it until moment of impact. Set up an automatic switch to throw in all power one minute before contact and to maintain it for—how long can the installation take boosted power, V ictor?"

"O n emergency overload about thirty minutes."

"For twenty-five minutes, Paul." It should be long enough. If not, a few minutes would serve no purpose, but to burn out the installation would leave them defenseless against normal dangers.

H elena had done her best to provide a safe-guard against the rest.

Koenig looked at the capsule she placed in his hand. It was large, smooth, brightly colored and he was reminded of a sugared almond, but the hard outer coating held not a nut but a chemical combination of involved complex ity. H e watched as she handed one to everyone in Main Mission.

A s she returned to face him, he said, "What is it, H elena?"

"A witches' brew." She shrugged at his ex pres-sion. "G uesswork, mostly, we've had had no time to make thorough tests, but it should help. Think of it as water which will damp down a fire. If things get too bad bite down on the coating, break it, the liq uid inside will be absorbed by the inner membranes and enter the bloodstream. A s I said, it should act like a deluge of water on a flame."

L ooking at his own capsule, Bergman said, "My guess is that it contains an anti-hallucinogenic coupled with a strong tranq uiliz er and maybe a curare derivative. A m I right?"

"A s much as you'd be right if you said that a house consisted of bricks, planks and plaster. D on't worry about what's in it, just takeit if you feel that you are losing control. You too, John."

"Yes, H elena."

"I mean it." She looked at his face, the curve of his eyebrows, the set of his jaw. A face which revealed his inner strength and determination. O ne she didn't want to see turned int a slack, idiotic mask as Ivor Khokol's had been. The man who now lay like a vegetable in Medical. "Take care, John."

"You too, H elena."

H er duties were with the sick, her place in the Section she commanded, and he watched her go, turning back to the Big Screen only after the doors had closed behind her.

"Nine," said Morrow. "Nine minutes to go."

"Sandra?"

"Still nothing, Commander."

Nothing to do but wait as the seconds dragged past, the hands of the chronometer swept around and around the illuminated dial, as the digital counters ripped to show a reducing number of figures. Minutes and seconds pouring through the sieve of time.

"Five seconds," breathed Bergman. "Three... two... one... "

Madness!

five

It came in a wave, a flood, a crashing deluge which tore at the fabric of reality and turned the familiar into the strange. The lights changed, the instruments became grimacing faces, the floor a stinking morass which sucked at the feet with a liq uid sq uelching. A nd, abruptly, each was alone.

D avid Kanosucked in his breath, feeling the fear of dreadful knowledge, the soul-twisting terror which urged him to run before it was too late. They were coming for him, he knew it, the tall and dreadful shapes with their makeshift uniforms and rifles, alongside pistols, machetes and knives, the instruments of pain and torment. The forest rustled with them, the light of their torches, ever-searching, limned the fleeing figures of boys whom they'd mold into soldiers, force into combat and servitude. Their faces were the modern eq uivalent of the tribal ghostmasks, the devil-masks, the depicted god-faces.

Men seeking to kill, to rape, to burn.

Men hating his people for what they were and what they had.

ROGUE PLANET

H e knew he would likely die at their hands. O r hidden beyond the limits of his village, there were animals which would take him and send his spirit shrieking from his flesh to linger in an everlasting agony.

H e crouched, trembling, the rattle of gunfire matching the pounding of his heart. H e could smell the stink of his own sweat, reminding him of his own fear. Beneath his naked feet the mud sucked at him like a living thing.

Behind him Computer reared to the sky. Computer—his obsession.

H e straightened and the gunfire became a rolling susurration, the leaping torchlight a ruby illumination painting the faces before him, rapt faces alive with awe and respect. Those who had come to kneel and worship at the base of the god and its priest. The god Computer and the priest Kano.

Kano the priest. H e Who L earned. H e Who Knew A ll Aswers. H e Who Served.

Turning he lifted his arms towards the rearing bulk of the god-machine. Behind him the worshippers sucked in their breaths, and the gunfire, more sonorous now, rolling with a relentless deliberation, boomed like distant thunder.

Computer was god. Computer knew all things. Computer was all-powerful. G reat was Computer's priest. G reat was Kano.

"Kano!" The shout lifted towards the stars. "Kano! Kano! Kano!"

The clash of spears and the throbbing of tribal drums, the racial memory of long-lost days, oiled bodies like ebon in the torchlight, paint, masks, blood—one who challenged.

"Kano!"

The law of the jungle—kill or die! "Kano!"

A n image of himself, tall, oiled, naked ex cept for paint, hands tipped with claws which reached to rip and tear. H is own hands reaching in turn, gripping, holding, his jaws open to bite.

Teeth closing to crunch on something brittle.

D arkness!

In Medical something stirred. A man who had turned into a vegetable and who now became a man again. Ivor Khokol sighed and lifted an arm and sat upright holding the reins of his horse, feeling the pound of its hooves as it carried him towards glory.

H e had slept, he thought, doz ing in the saddle, an old trick of the H iung when engaged on a long journey. Now he turned to look at the massed riders behind, a loose column which stretched back to the horiz on. They were heading south, to R ome, to the loot of the ancient world.

To the woman of his dreams.

She was tall and blonde and he had seen her face limned against the stars. From her he would gain fine sons, men-children who would grow into warriors and be an added strength to his arm. O nce he had been afraid of her, of the power she held, but that time was over and now she would crumple in his hands.

"O n!" H e yelled. "O n!"

H elen heard the cry.

She sat at her desk, motionless, even her eyes un-shifting in their sockets. In her bloodstream flowed a complicated mass of chemicals, a stronger combination than what she had given to the others, one whose efficiency she was now testing.

From an instrument before her a light winked at one-second intervals. R eality.

With the light came a high-pitched bleep. R eal-ity.

Two checks at least—if she could remember them. Two anchors to a familiar world. A pair of signposts which would remain unaffected by whatever mental storm might overwhelm her.

Now she stared at a light which burned con-tinuously, heard a sound without break.

L ike worms her thoughts crawled to match the observed phenomena.

"... time sense affected... disorientation of assoc ciated stimuli... no sense of physical contact with chair or desk... vision affected... bodily tempera ture seems higher than normal... metabolic change... hearing... "

"O n!" A harsh yell, repeated. "O n!"

Ivor Khokol riding with his warriors to the sack of R ome.

H e came running from the place in which she had left him to halt, staring, hands moving before him as if they held reins, body twitching to the motions of an invisible mount. L ike a child riding a hobby horse, she thought, and resisted the impulse to laugh.

What an amusing hallucination!

In turn, he saw a shimmer of gold. R ome!

In R ome was all the gold of the world and now ii was before him, lambent in the glowing sun, rich, inviting, waiting for him to touch it, to scoop it into his arms. D ismounting, he ran towards it, seeing it change to become a piled mass of delicate strands.

A change which left him unmystified all men knew of the magic owned by the ancient keepers of hallowed temples. A nd gold was gold no matter in what form it came.

H elena rose as he came forward, feeling her fragile defenses begin to crack, the chemical walls splinter, so that the world dissolved into a shower of shattered gems which filled the air with a smoking, scintillating kaleidoscope. Shapes became distorted, the desk turned into a crouching, snarling beast carved from obsidian, the walls vanished to be replaced by an endless vista of rolling plains, the roof became an emerald sky.

Khokol became a nightmare.

She backed from the sq uat, hairy, snarling thing which came towards her, hopping like a toad, webbed hands ex tended, bulging eyes glowing with a killer's rage. H er back hit something solid and she turned and saw a row of jars each containing a severed human head. Eyes watched her, unblinking, the whites of the balls veined with a tracery of red.

O n them spiders fed.

"No!" The sight was vile. D isgusting. "No!"

A   hand clawed at her side, ripped at her uniform, fingers touching her bared skin. A   fetid odor stung her nostrils and slime spattered her hair. Weight pulled at her, threw her to the ground, sent her sprawling, looking into the ridged and mottled face of a repulsive monstrosity.

"No!"

Pressure flattened her hips, forced apart her thighs, held her shoulders hard against the floor. The stench of rotting teeth filled her nostrils, the odor of suppuration and gangrene wafted about her, slime touched her, filth embraced her.

"No!"

O nce, ages ago, she had been attacked by craz ed degenerates while working in a hospital. They had intended murder. She had escaped then and hard-won ex perience came to her aid now. A scream followed the upward jerk of a knee. A nother, the stabbing action of her thumbs. A   third, followed by a liq uid gurgle, the savage chop of her stiffened hand.

The weight holding her fell away and she rose to run, to stand, to gasp while the universe spun around her.

The anchors!

Where were her anchors?

The light and the sound. The desk on which the instrument sat. The drugs which lay beneath housed in their air-powered hypodermic. R elease from the nightmare which held her, the madness in which she was lost.

Moving she tripped and fell, to rise sobbing, hands ex tended, groping as if blind. A flash and a high, thin note. A flash, a sound, another flash. A n eye winking... winking... winking...

Something like a dagger which hissed as she thrust it against her throat.

Koenig stirred, feeling the hardness beneath his cheek, the wetness on face and chin. There was a bitter, acrid taste in his mouth together with something sharp and jagged. H e spat it out, stirred, sat upright, his head swimming with a momentary nausea. Touching his chin, he found it thick with blood.

It had come from his nose and from a minor gash on his tongue, the result of the sharp coating of the capsule he had crushed beneath his teeth when, at the end, the battle for his sanity had been lost.

Sitting, eyes closed, head lowered to rest on his knees, he saw again the parade of nightmare.

The base a wreck, rooms shattered, panels splintered, the screens ripped free and hanging blind and dead. A s the personnel lay broken and lifeless all around. L ike a bereft ghost he had wandered through A lpha, seeing nothing but desolation, unable to understand why he alone had remained alive.

Pictures remained. Paul lying with his spine broken, one hand twitching, blood streaming from his parted lips. Kano, face distorted with the rictus of death, arms clutched around his precious machine. V ictor, froz en and pale. H elena

H e didn't want to remember how she had appeared.

H ow she could still appear.

"No!"

H e was dead and damned, alone in the ruin of his command, all he had ever held precious gone for all time, ruined, thrown away by his stubborn refusal to retreat, to withdraw, to return. The tears had stung his eyes even as he had fought the sickness mounting within him. Empty rooms and compartments, living q uarters looking like a shambles, red against the white, red against the green, red against blue and yellow and orange. R ed, red everywhere, a deluge of blood.

"No!" Even in memory it was too much and he shivered, fighting the sickness, feeling again the rage which had joined it, the killing fury against whoever or whatever had done this thing to him and to his people. "No!"

The windows had been shattered, the air gone, but he was still alive. The power had failed and shadows had accentuated the horror, grim shapes limned by the pale glow of the emergencies, yet he could feel the beat of light against his lids. H e had been hurt, dying, yet the wetness was only that of sweat and a little blood.

Koenig opened his eyes.

Bergman stared at him, his skull intact, both eyes in place, forehead bearing a familiar crease.

"John!" he said. "John! Thank G od!"

Koenig rose. A t his console Paul Morrow was shaking his head even as his fingers danced over his controls. Kano, looking a peculiar shade of grey beneath his brown skin, was at his position. H is eyes were bloodshot and scratches marked his cheeks, but his lips were free of the ugly smile Koenig remembered.

"Commander!" Sandra Benes, pale, fragile, looked like delicate porcelain. "You are alright. I thought— thank G od you are alright!"

"Paul?"

"It's over," said Bergman before Morrow could answer. "We've passed through whatever it was that caused those hallucinations. H elena's drug helped us. Without it I doubt if we could have survived. Even as it was, it—well, never mind. John?"

"I'm all right." Koenig wiped at his face then rubbed his smeared hand against his uniform. H e was still a little daz ed, still unable to fully grasp that the death and devastation he had seen had only been a nightmare. A n illusion. Something born of fear and the disorientation of his sensory apparatus. A nd something of the horror remained. "H elena!"

"She's all right, John." Bergman was q uick with his reassurance. "Paul has checked out Medical."

"I must talk to her." H is fingers were trembling too much and the commlock fell as he snatched it from his belt. "G et her on screen. Now!"

A moment and it was done, and Koenig felt a sudden relax ation as he looked at the pale face framed by the golden hair. Not dead, then. Not torn and ravaged, ripped and abused, left like a foul obscenity on the sterile floor. Not a ghastly travesty of the human form left in careful array, the art form of a diseased and degenerate beast.

"John?" H er eyes widened as she searched his face. "John—what is wrong?"

"Nothing. A re you all right?"

"Yes, but—"

"G et up here." D uty overrode inclination, the need to have her close, to reassure himself that what he had seen had truly been a hallucination. "Wait. Can Bob manage? H e can? G ood, then join me at once."

"But, John, I must—"

"Join me!"

A s he blanked the screen, Morrow said, "I can tell you what she wanted to report, Commander. Ivor Khokol went craz y and tried to kill her. She had to defend herself."

"A nd?" H ad the attack been the cause of his nightmare? H er fear somehow transmitted to his fevered brain? Sadistic images born of fear or received from her attacker? "A nd what, Paul? A n- swer me!"

"H e was dead when they found him."

Killed without intent, a victim of the general distortion—and how many others would have died had they not been locked away and safely drugged? Koenig drew in his breath and shook his

head. H e still felt daz ed, divorced from his surroundings, and he guessed that he had crushed
the capsule later than he should have done. The
others had obviously recovered before him and
appeared to be showing less of the effects of the
mind-distorting field through which they had
passed.

"H ere, John. It may help."

Silently he took the container of water Bergman handed to him, swallowing the pills which
accompanied it, washing them down together
with the acrid taste of chemicals and blood.

H elena appeared as the drug began to take effect. Q uickly she ex amined his face, wiped away
the blood and gave a tremulous smile.

"John, I must tell you. Something dreadful
happened and—"

"I know. Paul told me." H e stared at her, devouring her with his eyes. Tall, whole, clean, un-
hurt—thank G od it had only been an illusion!

"Base intact, no damage, all systems operational," reported Morrow from his console. "O ne
dead, and three with minor injuries—all self-
inflicted. D efense screens at optimum."

A nd nothing lay before them.

Koenig stared at the screens, seeing only what
had been visible before, the cold glitter of distant
stars, the fuz z of distant nebulae. They had
passed through hell and arrived—where? "Sandra?"

"Nothing, Commander. A �no, wait! I am re-
ceiving positive indications of a strong force-

emission lying directly ahead. Magnetic field of incredible density." She gave the figures and Bergman shook his head.

"A maz ing! Such firm control! D o you realiz e what this means, John? A neat total restraining of all leakage. O bviously, the outer barrier through which we have passed utiliz ed any seepage of energy to power the psychic force-field which serves as a warning and defense. H ow far, Sandra?"

"Close." She looked up, her face strained. "We should reach it within two minutes."

"Full boost on defensive shield!" snapped Koenig. "Sound the red alert. A ctivate all ex ternal scanners."

H e felt H elena at his side and took her hand in his own, his fingers firm against the warmth of her skin. H e caught the scent of her perfume, a delicate floral aroma, and a strand of her golden hair caressed his cheek.

"The transition point," murmured Bergman. "This is where all light and radiation are seiz ed by the enveloping forces and rotated in a half-circle. If we were a photon of light or even a minute particle of spatial debris, we too could be so rotated."

But the Moon had tremendous mass and any force which could move it so q uickly from its destined path would volatiz e the entire body to incandescent vapor.

"John!" whispered H elena. "John, I"

"Now!"

ROGUE PLANET

The screens blurred as Bergman called out, stars seeming to flow from the center to the edges, to wink, to vanish...

To be replaced by a wall of utter darkness.

A blank, ebon surface which served as a backdrop to something incredible.

"John!" H elena's fingers dug into his hand, the nails gouging at his flesh. "John—it's a brain! A living, human brain!"

s i x

It shone with a pulsating greenish glow, a leprous luminescence blotched with the lines of convolutions, divided into sponge-like hemispheres, rounded and soft-looking and incredible.

"A brain!" Bergman's voice reflected his amaz ement. "But big! So big!"

The siz e of the Moon as seen from Earth, te-mendous, dominating. Koenig stared at it, noting details unseen before, the haz elike appearance of the thing, the blurred detail, the pulse of the greenish glow. The image blurred even more as he watched.

"Paul?"

"Interference, Commander. The ex ternal san-ners are being affected by the discharge from our defensive shield." H is voice rose a little, "D is-charge far higher than normal. A radiated loss of seven percent and mounting."

Koenig moved his eyes and stared at the ex - ternal view of the screen. The surface was glow-ing, bright with emitted energy, scintillating with eye-hurting brilliance.

"Sandra—any sign of anything approaching?"

"No, Commander."

ROGUE PLANET

No attacking vessels, then, and it would do no harm to drop the shield. The image in the main screens cleared as Morrow collapsed the shield, sharpening in detail, shining with an inner light, an emerald mystery.

It couldn't be a brain. Not a human, pulsating, living organ—the siz e alone was against it being that. Koenig listened as Sandra Benes reported the findings of her instruments.

"Mass 2 .3 6 5 L unar. V olume 5 .4 6 3 . D is .0 2 5 au. L ocal radiation 7 .97 3 plus normal. Temperature—" she broke off, then said unsteadily, "apparently z ero."

"Check!"

"I have done that, Commander. O ur instruments must be defective in some way. No lightsource can have z ero temperature and yet that is what we appear to be looking at."

A mystery, another to add to the rest, but the solutions could wait. Koenig's first responsibility was to the base and he listened as the reports came in.

"A ll systems operating. No damage. A lpha at optimum." Morrow turned in his chair. "Stand down from R ed A lert, Commander?"

"Yes. Switch to Yellow. What do you make of it, V ictor?"

Bergman was already at work with his circular slide rules, his computer terminal and other apparatus.

"A moment, John. Kano, will you please check this analogue with Computer? Thank you." H e pursed his lips as the technician handed him the readout. "A s I suspected. Interesting. Most interesting."

Koenig said tightly, "No games, V ictor. I want answers."

"We have passed through the outer wall of force isolating this area from the normal universe. Naturally the parameters are dark because no light is being received—all is being rotated around the circumference of this space. We are, fortunately, travelling on a line which will bisect the sphere on a chord towards its lower region. I say ' fortunately', because if we had been travelling in a more direct line towards the center, then a collision with the central mass would have been inevitable." Bergman made an adjustment on his rule and frowned at the result. "A t our velocity and knowing the relative masses of the two bodies both would have been totally shattered."

The death and devastation the warning had meant?

"A nd?"

"Be a little patient, John. We have, in effect, entered a completely new universe and it will take a little time to learn something about it. A fter all, we have taken two million years to learn about our own and still are ignorant."

"Please, V ictor, no lectures. Can you anticipate any immediate danger?"

"Immediate? No."

"Conclusions?"

ROGUE PLANET

Bergman sighed and shook his head. "You ask a hard q uestion, John, and I can only give the roughest of answers. Basically, we should, if conditions are as we know, merely proceed, until eventually we leave this area as we entered it. Imagine a circle. Imagine an object, the tip of a pen, for ex ample. It moves on a straight line, hits one side of the circle, passes on, crosses the area and leaves the ring on the far side. We are the tip of the pen and this space is the circle."

O ne containing the tremendous representation of a human brain. Koenig glanced at it where it hung in the screens, grotesq ue, monstrous, and knew himself to be the victim of suggestion and illusion.

The thing could not be a human brain.

It just couldn't be at all.

The color was wrong—a brain would have been grey and streaked with red, not a pulsating green. H elena had planted the suggestion, forming an association with a familiar object, turning a vague similarity into a firm depiction. The dark lines of assumed convolutions must be fissures and valleys, the green that of vegetation, the apparent pulsation a fault in the scanners, the glow—?

"Sandra—still no temperature?"

"None that we are registering, Commander."

Cold light? It was possible. Some insects had the facility of producing a glow by chemical means, but Koenig knew that nothing radiating that brightly could possibly do it without emitting energy of some kind. A nd that energy would register as heat.

"Check on the complete electromagnetic spectrum. Kano, feed all received data into Computer for the purpose of constructing a local analogue of our present and ex trapolated situation. A nything new as yet, Paul?"

"Findings being correlated, Commander." Morrow grew busy with his instruments. "A dditional data on screens now." The image of the glowing central mass shifted and something else took its place. "This was behind the main body and has just come into view."

It was a ball of something which could have been rock, but the surface was rounded, smooth, a dull grey illuminated by the green glow and resembling a polished pebble. A natural satellite of the central mass, perhaps, but Koenig didn't think so.

Bergman had an alternative answer.

"It could have been trapped sometime in the past. G iven enough time other objects besides ourselves must have entered this pocket universe. That could have been a lump of stellar debris at one time, a small planetoid or a large meteor."

"Trapped," said Koenig. "H ow? Why? If it entered, then why didn't it leave?"

"There could be many reasons," said Bergman precisely. "It could have had a low relative velocity. It could have bisected this space very near the central mass and have been caught by its gravitational attraction. O ♁"

ROGUE PLANET

Koenig snapped, "Kano! H ave Computer check on those possibilities."

"John?" Bergman frowned. "Is something on your mind?"

"Never take the obvious for granted, V ictor. You were one of the first to teach me that. Just because an answer appears to be the logical solution doesn't mean that it is correct. Kano?"

"The possibilities mentioned by Professor Bergman are mutually conflicting." D avid Kano cleared his throat as he studied the readout. "A s-suming the relative masses to be the same as at present observed, the difference in relative velocity would have had to be small for the intruder to be trapped into a stable orbit. But if it had been so low, then it would have been drawn by gravitational attraction into the main body."

"In other words," said Koenig grimly, "if the intruder was moving slow enough to be trapped, then it wouldn't have been moving fast enough to avoid destruction. So much for logical answers, V ictor. Want to try again?"

Bergman said slowly, "There's another answer, but we don't know enough yet about local conditions to be sure if it is correct. I hope that it isn't."

"Why?"

"This could be a closed system, John. A miniature universe with its own laws and own energy levels which have little relation to those with which we are familiar. In that case—" H e paused, then said bleakly, "It could be that everything entering this space is trapped. We could go on and on, but all we'd be doing is following the interior of this space around and around. If that is the case, then we are caught—trapped for eternity!"

Bob Mathias adjusted the microscope, stared through the eyepiece, made a further adjustment and, after another ex amination, leaned back from the instrument. H e was frowning, twin lines graven deep between his eyes, the corners of his mouth downturned a little as if he had looked at something unpleasant.

"D octor?" Nurse Sinto halted at his side. She was trim and neat in her uniform, olive skin enhanced by the stark whiteness of her sleeve. "You look upset. Is something wrong?"

"I'm not sure."

"Not to be sure is to be aware of life," she smiled. "O nly the dead can be certain of the absence of change."

"Which is an apparent contradiction as you know. In death, there can be no certainty."

"True," admitted the girl. "A nd with only one hand, how can there be clapping?"

Mathias shook his head. A t times he found the girl impossible. Young, attractive, A vril Sinto seemed to take a delight in firing abstruse q uotations at him, many of which he was fairly certain she invented on the spot, but she was, he had to admit, a superb master of her trade, and for that he could tolerate much.

A nd he liked her. L iked her, perhaps, a little too much.

ROGUE PLANET

"A vril—"

"Bob?" H e had broken the coldly formal manner of professional address, and she reminded
him of it with the use of his given name and a
smile. "Were you going to invite me to join you
after duty? I've a recording of G us H alliday's ' L u-
nar A pproach,' remember it? The one with the
simulated rocket blast and the sub-audible voices?
If you want, you could come to my q uarters and
listen to it."

"Thank you, A vril, but no."

"D on't you like good music?"

"G ood music, yes." H e softened his rejection.
"You know the wise old saying? O ne man's meat
is another's poison? G us H alliday may be a good
musician to you but to me he's a—"

"Careful, Bob!" she warned with mock ferocity.
"You're talking of the man I could have loved. But
I know what you mean. To be honest I borrowed
the recording because I thought you might like it.
Now I've found we have yet another thing in
common. Well, what else can we do? I know!
Take me to the observation room. I've heard the
view now is fantastic. Is it true that D octor R ussell
first described the central body as a brain?"

"I don't know. I wasn't in Main Mission at the
time."

"Well, it is. Nurse Wong told me. She's seen it.
A brain, Bob. Think of it. A planet ed brain."

"O r something which just happens to resemble
one," he corrected. "A walnut looks the same only
much smaller. That's why the R omans used to

think it good for headaches and such. The similarity of appearance made them think the two were connected in the same way." H e sighed, wistfully, "Medicine in those days was simple."

"H it and miss, Bob. If it worked you did it again. Now we know ex actly what we're doing and why."

"D o we?" H is shrug was ex pressive. "I wish I could be as sure."

She caught his tone, recogniz ing its seriousness, and immediately became the true professional she was. The time for informality had passed.

"There is something wrong! What is it, D octor?"

"I'm not sure. Perhaps nothing more than a contaminated culture. I've been checking blood corpuscles and noted something strange. Then I checked out a culture of bacteria, X 2 3 8 harmless but essential component of the lower bowel."

"A nd?"

"Probably nothing. It could even be fatigue. In any case I'll have to check again. If you could prepare two cultures for me, nurse?"

"X 2 3 8 ?"

"Yes."

"Both on agar?"

She moved away as he nodded and, alone, he turned again to the microscope. L ost in the magnified world of subcultures, he didn't hear H elena approach him. O nly when she rested her hand on his shoulder did he lift his head.

"What? O h, D octor R ussell!"

"D id I startle you?"

"No—I wasn't ex pecting you. H ow is Jackson?"

"H e'll be all right." Jackson was one of those who had recently injured himself. "Some superficial bruising, minor contusions, but the fractured ribs we suspected turned out to be little more than hairline breaks." H elena glanced at the notes Mathias had made. "Blood-checks, Bob?"

"A routine count. Sanderson is still under electro-sleep, but he's healing, slowly. I'm more concerned about Ellman. H e isn't recovering as he should, and I suspect a lowered red-cell count."

"Ellman?" H elena frowned. "H e was discharged as fit before we hit the barrier. Before—" she swallowed, then forced herself to continue— "before Ivor Khokol collapsed."

"Yes." Mathias removed the slide from the instrument and selected another. "You remember how concerned we were at Sanderson's prolonged hospitaliz ation. H is wound seemed reluctant to heal. Well, I've been doing some research on the problem, no answer as yet and maybe there never will be, but I did bump into something odd when I tested out Ellman's blood. H e was injured about the same time and suffered the same superficial conditions. Well— look at this."

H e stepped aside as H elena stooped over the microscope. For a long moment she ex amined the slide. "A nd?"

"Now ex amine this."

"A comparison?"

She turned at his nod and again became engrossed in her study of the illuminated picture beneath the lenses. Without speaking she selected other slides, then looked at his notes.

"You made other tests, Bob?"

"O n X 2—they check out." H e drew in his breath and held it for a moment before releasing it in an audible sigh. "I'm having fresh cultures made, of course, but I'm afraid the picture is clear."

H elena looked at him, a skilled man, an ex perienced physician and a master of pathology. Not a man to be easily terrified and not one to show unfounded anx iety. A nd far too good a scientist to leap to unfounded assumptions.

Yet she had to know. G ently she said, "You suspect disease, Bob?"

"You saw."

"I saw, yes, but I want you to say it. You have done the tests and made the conclusions. I ask you again, Bob. D isease?"

"No," he said. "A ge."

The observation room was fitted with chairs and soft coverings with a fountain giving off a musical tinkling, a susurration of subdued melody designed to give the impression of warmth and security, the balmy magic of a summer's evening, a scented, subtropical night.

H ere lovers came to walk beneath the stars, to sit and whisper sweet promises. H ere too came the tired and those who felt the need to stretch the vision into the infinite. A nd here too came artists and poets seeking inspiration, those who felt the need to be alone, others who wished to cherish memories of a vanished age.

From a shadowed place against one curved wall Koenig looked at dimly seen heads, saw the glimpses of arms and legs, the pale blur of lifted faces, other faces, darker, gleaming like ebony, like sun-kissed fruit. If any saw him they gave no sign and he, in turn, stood as if he were a man in total isolation.

That, too, was an attribute of the room. In it, should that be the desire, privacy was absolute.

A privacy now invaded by the watchful eye of the alien sun.

Words, he thought, ones which had little meaning and which, even so, were wrong. The thing was not a sun and it was far from alien. H ere, in this plane, it belonged and A lpha did not. The Moon was the intruder. They were the alien interlopers.

A nd they would remain ken—but for how long?

A gain, Koenig stared at the enigmatic, brain like core of the central mass. Its greenish radiation pulsed as if in response to the pounding of a living heart. Its shape, all the more disq uieting because of medical associations, gave it the appearance of a monstrosity. Its satellite, unseen now, had vanished behind the main body which hung low above the horiz on. A n accident had made it so; had they entered the mysterious area at a slightly different angle, then it would have appeared directly overhead.

L ifting the commlock from his belt, Koenig triggered the instrument and read the digital time-check thrown on the tiny screen.

It vanished as he pressed a stud. "V ictor?"

"John!" Bergman was in his private laboratory, seated, a litter of graphs and papers before him. "Where are you?" H e nodded as Koenig answered. "Waiting?"

"Yes. H ow much longer?"

"Without precise measurements we have to allow for a wide margin of error. A nd, as you know, we had trouble in determining the area of this space. Even now we have only a rough approx i-mation."

"H ow long?"

"You'll know as soon as we find out, John. D on't ask for the impossible."

A stubborn man, thought Koenig as the screen went blank. But a less stubborn one would have been dead long ago, and certainly without that trait Bergman would never have achieved his fame. For that, if nothing else, he should be respected.

But it was hard to wait.

H ard to hang on the edge of a precipice of doubt, not knowing if a simple matter of time would solve their problem by showing there was no problem at all, or whether the hopes and entire lifestyle of the base would have to be changed.

For if they were trapped, change would be inevitable.

The commlock hummed and he looked at Sandra's smooth and lovely face.

"Commander! We have determined—"

"Wait! I'm coming to join you. H ave Professor Bergman notified."

H e was already in Main Mission when Koenig arrived, standing to one side of the console, his face heavy with deeply graven lines. A n ex pression which told Koenig the worst.

"We're trapped?"

"I—yes, John. I'm afraid so."

"Kano?"

"Computer verifies, Commander. O ur measured distance from the central body is remaining static. Sufficient time has elapsed for our velocity to have carried us away from it, if we were continuing to move in a straight line relative to this area."

"But how?" Koenig frowned as he snapped the q uestion. "O ur relative mass is too great for us to have been caught by gravitational attraction. A nd our velocity was too high for us to be swung into orbit so soon."

"In our own universe you would be right," said Bergman. "But, as I warned, the rules here are not the same as those outside. D irection, velocity, mass—all have different meanings. A nd there's something more. Sandra?"

"A ll surface instrument readings are betraying an ex tremely odd condition, Commander. There is an increasing amount of energy potential radiating from the Moon and apparently streaming into space."

"What?" Koenig glared his incredulity. "Energy leaving the surface?"

"Yes."

"That doesn't make sense. We should be receiving it from the sun—the main body. It's radiating light and there must be other energy emissions. Yet you say—Paul?"

"Monitors confirm, Commander. The base is suffering a continual energy loss."

"Scale?"

"Treble normal and mounting."

"Cause?"

"A s yet unknown, but we have a clue." Morrow killed the lights, leaving only the screens and monitors active. H is face, reflecting the glow of telltales, took on the aspect of a clown's mask, patches of colored luminescence moving in a drifting pattern of variegated hue. "L ook at the O mphalos, Commander."

"The O mphalos?"

"The central body—we had to give it a name and this seemed appropriate."

The O mphalos—the center. Koenig looked at it, bright with greenish light, marked, pulsating.

"I'm boosting the registers," said Morrow. "L ifting the reception monitors into the ultraviolet and beyond and incorporating a compensatory translator. Now watch!"

ROGUE PLANET

The image flickered as he threw switches, the greenish hue changing to a pale violet.

"A beam!" In the shadowed darkness Bergman echoed his amazement. "We're connected by a beam!"

s ev en

It rose all around, an inverted cone of shimmering radiance which led from the Moon to a point on the O mphalos. A funnel of sharply defined clarity which joined the two bodies together as a line would join a hooked fish to a rod.

Koenig felt his muscles tighten at the analogy.

"What is this? A freak of some kind? Sandra?"

She too was touched with colored patches of shifting brightness, reds and blues, greens and yellows from the banked instruments before her touching uniform, hair, face and hands.

"The registers show a directional flow of energy along the beam from us to the O mphalos, Commander. It checks with the observed drain."

"V ictor?" Koenig turned, starig into the darkness, feeling a mounting irritation, one caused by his hampered vision. "Paul, turn on the lights." H e blinked as Morrow obeyed. "Well, V ictor?"

Bergman said slowly, "We can make assumptions, John, but we need more facts. We know that the beam did not originate with us, so it is safe to assume that it came from the O mphalos. It could be a natural effect of this space, an automatic discharge-reception such as the ex change of energy between a particle of low potential and one of high. Something similar to a lightning flash, for ex ample."

"A flash is almost instantaneous."

"True, but we could be dealing with a temporal vagary—time could appear or actually be different here. In that case, an almost instantaneous flash would seem to us to be of long duration."

"You're guessing, V ictor." Koenig looked at the computer. "Kano—can you do better?"

"Not me, Commander, but Computer—maybe."

"Try. Find out degrees of probability and waste no time about it. Paul, check every inch of that space out there you can with everything you've got. I want—" Koenig broke off as one of the screens flashed then went blank. "Trouble?"

"A n ex ternal scanner burned out." Morrow made checks and drew in his breath with a sharp inhalation. "I should have guessed this would happen. The energy drain is affecting our ex ternal installations. That particular scanner was close to the defense screen. When it radiated as it did, it must have weakened the components, and the prevailing drain finished the job."

"A nd the others?"

"A lready show loss of conversion efficiency, Commander."

"H ave them replaced—all of them. G et on to Maintenance right away. V ictor—come with me."

In his office Koenig sealed the doors cutting him from Main Mission and slumped at his desk.

Bergman took a seat facing him and for a moment they looked at each other.

"It's bad, V ictor. R ight?"

"It could be, John."

"It is." Koenig was certain of it, in his heart, head and stomach. The physical signs of an intuition honed by repeated dangers. "That beam— natural or not it's got us hooked. Maybe that's why we took up an orbit around the O mphalos. That other satellite too, perhaps?" H e punched a button and looked at Morrow's face as it appeared on the communications post. "Paul—a q uestion. D oes the planetoid we observed also have a beam connecting it to the O mphalos?"

"It's just come into view, Commander. If you'll hold—" A pause. Then, "Yes, it does."

"Thank you." Koenig broke the connection and, rising, began to pace the floor. "A n ex planation," he said. "V ictor, give me an explanation."

"A s yet we can only guess, John."

"Then let me make a start. H ere we have a closed system, an area of space which is sealed against the reception of any form of ex ternal energy. A ny radiated forms, that is. We ourselves are proof that matter can penetrate. R ight?"

Bergman nodded.

"Such an area would, in time, reach entropic death. A ll energy would have reached a common level and there would be no differing potentials. No life of any kind could ex ist in such a space, no matter, nothing but a sea of diffused and low-level residue of energy."

ROGUE PLANET

"There is an alternative," said Bergman. "A remote possibility that all available energy would become concentrated into a common node. There would still be a rundown, naturally, but instead of a sea of low-order residue there would be a—for want of a better word—a lump of inert mass. A sh, in essence."

"A magnet," said Koenig. "A sponge which would grab every particle of energy that was going. Sucking it into itself like dry ground sucks water. It caught that planetoid and who knows what else besides? Now it's caught us," he added bitterly. "Swinging us like an apple on the end of a string. We're trapped in this damned bubble in the sky. Whoever or whatever placed those warnings knew what they were talking about."

"D eath and devastation," said Bergman bleakly. "D eath and devastation."

The loss of all energy, the reduction of matter itself, the end of A lpha and all it contained.

Inevitable—unless *somehow* they could break free.

The Eagles rose like ungainly wasps, insect-like with the forward direct vision ports, their armor a natural chitin, their command modules the thorax , the passenger compartments the abdomens. Their lasers vicious stings.

Carter, in command of Eagle O ne, led the other two up and away from the Moon. Below the base rested, as if deserted, the buildings masked, the launching pads now empty. H igher and he caught a flash of movement, tiny, suited figures almost invisible against the bleak L unarscape, dimly lit by the greenish luminescence of the O m-phalos.

"Surface techs," said his co-pilot. Frank D ale was young, eager, a little too loq uacious, but at least he was not a dreamer as Khokol had been. "A hell of a job—who wants to work on the ground?"

"Someone has to do it."

"Sure, just as someone has to do the cooking," agreed D ale. "I'm just glad that it isn't me."

Carter said tersely, "Check your instrumenta-tion."

"Sure, Skipper. A ll systems in the green."

"Keep them that way." The pilot pressed a control. "R eport in, Eagles Two and Three. A n-drews?"

"Everything smooth, Skipper."

"Torens?" Carter nodded as a second voice re-ported that all was well. It should be, all Eagles were kept at the optimum pitch of efficiency, but only a fool would take anything for granted in space. "R ight. Stay in position." A nother switch and Morrow looked from the screen.

"A lan?"

"A ll set to go. A ny alteration in conditions?"

"No. You'd best approach from the side away from the beam. It might be best to leave one Ea-gle in space in case of—"

"L eave it to me, Paul. I'm the one doing the job."

A nd risking his neck. Morrow caught the implication and shrugged. "So you are, A lan. D id I say you weren't?"

"In as many words—no."

"So why get annoyed?"

"I'm not." Carter shook his head. "I'm edgy, I guess. Sorry, Paul."

"For what?" Morrow returned Carter's smile. "It's all yours, A lan. H appy landings."

"Thanks."

Carter broke the connection and, as the screen went blank, lifted his eyes to stare through the forward vision ports. Their objective lay ahead, the smooth, slightly glistening ball of the planetoid he was to investigate.

It grew larger as their engines ate the space between them, the dull gleam a little more pronounced, but the surface showing no sign of detail. Carter led the flight towards the side away from the O mphalos, staying all clear of the cone he knew connected the two bodies, wary of any stress-fields which might be in the vicinity.

"A ndrews?"

"Skipper?"

"You stay in space and maintain observation of immediate area behind and to all sides. Torens, you hover low but free and keep us on your screens. R eport to Main Mission on regular schedule. U ndestood?"

H e smiled at the double agreement, one backed with envy, the other with resignation.

"D on't be jealous, Torens, you'll get your chance. You too, A ndrews. R ight, full alert we're going in."

Ten minutes later Carter stood on one of the strangest surfaces he had ever known.

It was smooth, that was the most overpowering impression, a ball of rock which had been ground in a gigantic lathe or set to tumble in a drum filled with other objects as large and as hard, so that common attrition would wear them into a near-perfect ball. A fantasy which lasted for only a moment. Then, as D ale came from the grounded Eagle towards him, Carter stooped to kneel, to thrust his helmet close to the ground and to run his gloved hands over the spot before his eyes.

"Skipper?"

"Move three paces to one side and take a sample." A s the copilot obeyed, Carter spoke again, this time on relay to where Morrow sat in Main Mission. "Paul? You read me?"

"Yes, go ahead."

"We've landed and I'm on the surface. It is smooth like a pebble which has been polished. No sign of fusing or of any corrosive forces."

"A ppearance general?"

"Yes. I'm taking samples and will investigate further."

Carter rose to his feet and stretched, feeling the slight chafe of the suit against his limbs. The enclosing helmet blocked his vision a little so that he had to turn his entire body to see towards the sides, arch his back to stare upwards.

"D ale, I'm heading towards the right of the Eagle. D ump the sample and follow."

H e would be ahead but there was no danger of getting lost. Nothing could hide in such a smooth ex panse, devoid as it was of tree or shrub or even a loose boulder. L ike an ant he moved over the sharply curving surface, eyes following the beam of his helmet light as it threw a cone of brilliance before him.

A light which showed a greyness striated with streaks of dull color, rusty, puce, brown, ochre, madder, indigo, ebony—ebony?

Carter paused and turned and looked again at the black patch which had caught his eye. It rested in a ragged circle a little to one side, the light penetrating it to show walls of a dark olive. A shaft?

"Skipper?" The co-pilot had caught up with him, breathing heavily as though he had been running. "What's that? A tunnel?"

"Maybe it's only a natural fissure."

"Maybe." D ale dropped to his knees at the edge of the opening. "H ey! It's got grips attached. Metal hoops by the look of it. We can climb down." H e added anx iously, "We are going to take a look, aren't we?"

They had come to investigate—what else?

Carter led the way, hands gripping the metal hoops which were set too far apart for comfort and too thick for an easy hold. O nce his boot slipped and he hung suspended by one hand, until he managed to find another hold and to take the strain off his aching shoulders. Below him was nothing but darkness, the beam of his helmet light seeming to be absorbed by the dull olive of the interior of the shaft. A bove, blocked by D ale's body, the ragged circle of the opening grew smaller.

Then a hoop broke and Carter was falling.

"D ale! I" H e landed before he could complete the warning, boots jarring, knees buckling as he dropped to roll, to land hard against a firm surface. A short fall, luckily, frightening in its sheer unex pectedness.

"Skipper? A re you all right?"

"Yes, but watch it. There's a broken hoop. Found it?"

"I—yes. There are others below still intact."

"G ood. Follow them. It can't be far to the bottom."

A blur of light and D ale was beside him, breathing a little heavily, leaning back to shine his light back up the shaft.

"O ne broken, Skipper. You were unlucky, but we'll have no trouble climbing back when we want." The light moved, the bright circle settling on an opening piercing the shaft. "A passage'.

O ne ten feet high, the walls rounded, smoothly finished and, like the shaft, of a dull olive. Carvings marked it, abstruse diagrams which could have been mere accident or deliberate decoration.

Touching them, D ale mused, "I've seen some-thing like this before, Skipper. In a museum one time. They came from Egypt. I forget what they were called."

"H ieroglyphics."

"What?"

"Picture writing."

"Writing?" D ale sucked in his breath. "What the hell do we have here?"

"I don't know," said Carter flatly. "But we can try to find out."

The passage curved, fell in a gentle slope, straightened to curve again in a reverse arc to what it was before. Twice Carter halted and at-tempted to contact the Eagles outside, both times without success.

"Try contacting the relay," he ordered. "My ra-dio isn't working."

"I can hear you."

"The other freq uency. The set may have been damaged when I fell." H e waited, then snapped, "Well?"

"Nothing." D ale's voice held a shrug. "Maybe that olive stuff's a barrier of some kind. What is it anyway? Metal of some kind?"

Carter struck at it with one of the tools clipped to his belt. The edge barely scratched the surface. H e tried again, using more force this time, then replaced the tool. Metal or not, the stuff was harder than rock and more stubborn than a tem-pered alloy.

D ale said. "Skipper, do we go on?"

A decision, and Carter knew he had to make it. Safety dictated that he should return, set up a relay point, then recommence the investigation only after making certain that all possible precautions had been made. But D ale, impatient, was already moving down the passage.

For a moment longer Carter hesitated. The matter was urgent, to return and summon the others would take precious time and probably be a waste. This passage would end soon and then would be the time to make decisions.

"Wait!" Carter stepped after the other man. "D ale, not so fast!"

"L ook!" The man had halted to stare at an engraved design. "L ook at that, Skipper! If that isn't a schematic of a rocket engine, I'll eat my helmet! A nd this an electronic circuit?"

A ccidents, the both of them, a trick of light and an overactive imagination, but there were resemblances and certainly the shaft and passage showed the impact of a sophisticated technology. Someone or something must have built them both, and those same people or things could have graced the bare walls with their concept of decoration.

"L et's see what lies lower down." D ale forged ahead, grunted as the passage forked, unhesitatingly took the left-hand corridor.

"Wait!" Carter swore as the other made no answer. "D ale, blast you, wait!"

The man had gone, racing ahead, following fancied discoveries, moving on before Carter could catch up with him. Turn after turn, the corridors branching, forking, each exactly alike, forming a maze in which Carter realized, too late, they were lost.

"Dale!" He lunged ahead, caught the man's shoulder, and pulled him back to slam him hard against the wall. "You fool! Why don't you answer me?"

He saw the startled face beyond the faceplate of the helmet, the moving lips. Metal rang in his ears as he jammed his own helmet against that of his co-pilot.

"Now can you hear me?"

"I—yes. What's the matter, Skipper? The radio—"

"Doesn't work. Or doesn't seem to be working. Check and report. Now!" Carter moved back, lifting his helmet, breaking contact, the bridge over which sound vibration had passed. Again he saw the lips move, but his speakers carried nothing but a soft hum. "Blast!"

The radios were out, but the silence could be broken. Suits were designed to cater to emergencies and, at times, radio silence was an advantage when too many men were working in an electronically "noisy" situation. Carter plucked at his belt, caught the terminal and unreeled the wire from its spool. Plugging it in to Dale's receptor, he said, "Better now?"

"Fine." The man sighed his pleasure at again being in vocal contact. "Wonder what killed the radios?"

A q uestion which could wait for an answer. The battery-powered direct connection was, in effect, a telephone and would serve. The nex t thing to do was to get out of the maz e of tunnels.

"This must be an old mine of some kind," mused D ale. "O r an underground bunker. I've seen pictures of bomb shelters and this could be one. Those diagrams could be maps of various sectors and storerooms." H si arm lifted to point. "That could be one, Skipper. To me it looks like a door."

The man had sharp eyes. Carter ex amined the spot, seeing the thin lines tracing an octagonal area, a sunken point containing a knurled wheel surrounded by a ring of individual designs. A combination lock? If so, it had to be built by al- iens, but all races which used doors and a means to lock them would follow a basic pattern. A nd unless there were stringent precautions against the practice, it might have been as common for them as it was for those of his own kind to make a note of the combination somewhere close.

H e found it seven feet from the edge of the door, three symbols which matched those found in the array around the knurled wheel. It moved beneath his gloved hands, turning, a nub halting at each of the symbols in turn. A guess-and Carter glowed at his success.

"You've done it!" D ale stepped forward as the door swung open. "Skipper, let's look inside!"

They stepped into a mausoleum.

Carter halted, D ale at his side, head and back tilted so as to look up and around. From the high, domed roof hung a mass of delicate, lace-like webs, sheets of fine gossamer glowing with re-fracted color, hues which faded to burn again, only to fade as they shifted the beams of their helmet lights. H anging in the webs, folded in it, were tall, fragile shapes with long, pointed skulls and narrow shoulders. The faces were peaked, the eyes enormous beneath protruding brows, the hands long-fingered with nails of pearl. Each hand held seven fingers and each finger was jointed in four places.

"D ead!" whispered D ale. "They're all dead."

They had been dead for eons. Even as they watched, a body fell from where it hung suspend-ed in the web which had served as a shroud, bones shattering to add their substance to the pile below, a heap of greyish dust which rose beneath the impact to settle in a slightly wider pattern.

The floor was covered with the dust, the ac-cumulated debris of ages.

"Webs." D ale moved, guiding his light, the cir-cle of brilliance probing the rear of the cavern. "Spiders, maybe?"

"No."

"Why not?"

"L ook at the bodies. None touched or eaten. Those webs weren't spun by spiders."

Not unless the bodies now suspended had stemmed from an arachnid ancestry, the ex tra limbs absorbed as mankind had absorbed the gills it had once known, shed the tail it no longer needed. A nd who could tell of the customs and ways of an alien race? They had lived and built and tried to survive with tunnels and sealed chambers and, perhaps, mystic signs scratched on the adamantine walls of their defenses. They had failed and had withdrawn to spend the last moments of their lives in communion with each other, gathering to fashion their webs, to hang in them, to die in them.

Their eq uivalent of beds, perhaps, of couches. O fombs.

Carter moved a little, looking at a pathetic tableau, two adult shapes together with two smaller ones of uneq ual siz e. A family group gathere together for mutual comfort? The hands were interlocked, the huge eyes open, pale and desiccated orbs which once, perhaps, had known the bitterness of tears.

"Skipper?" D ale was uneasy. "This place is giving me the creeps. H ow about getting the hell out of here?"

A nother body fell as he spoke, landing close by to dissolve into dust, adding more bulk to the powder which littered the floor. A nother, two at a time, a sudden fall of withered fingers like a ghastly rain.

"The floor! It's moving!" Carter turned towards the entrance. "The door! It's closed!"

More than the floor had moved. The slight tremor had swung the door on its gimbals sending it to fit snugly into the opening.

ROGUE PLANET

Even before he reached it Carter knew that somehow, it had locked itself.

That he and D ale were sealed in with the alien dead.

ei g h

Tony Ellman staggered and almost fell, regaining his balance with a tremendous effort, uneasily aware of the jagged rocks at his feet, the danger of smashing his face-plate, of dying in the airless void.

"Tony?" Nyat Cheng's concerned voice came from the radio. "You all right?"

"Fine."

"You sure?"

"Sure, I'm sure!" A nger edged his reply. Why the hell couldn't Cheng mind his own business? The day he needed mothering would be the day. "I'm fine," he said again. "Now let's q uit worrying about me and get on with the job. R ight?"

"Maybe you should report back in?"

"No!"

"I think you should." The overseer's voice held determination. "G et back to the bug, Tony, and take it easy. That's an order."

"You know what you can do with it?"

"Now you listen—"

"No! You listen! This is an emergency job, right? It needs to be done and fast—that's what emergency means. Now you stick to your job and let me get on with mine." H e added grimly, "I mean it, Nyat. Come near me and I'll brain you, and that goes for anyone else who thinks I'm getting past it."

A challenge and a stupid ne—why had he given it? Would he really fight if anyone came close? O nly an idiot would attempt to struggle outside on the L unar plain, when too many little things could cause a ruptured suit and burst lungs. But why the hell couldn't they leave him alone?

H e sighed, rising to straighten his back, conscious of the ache, the drag of weary muscles. D amn the hospital and the doctors-he hadn't felt right since they'd done that follow up series of tests on him after that second wave of craz iness when G reg tried to commit suicide. A nd that was another thing. G reg would never have done that. H e must have been affected by that whatever it was. A nd they should have been looking after him. G reg was one of the best. Who knew how long it would be before he was back on duty—*if* they allowed him back on duty. H e missed him.

Irritably, Ellman shook his head. What was the matter with him? Maybe G reg wanted to check out, and if so—so what? That was his business. Everyone had to die and some had the luck to go early and others had to wait. What you lost one way you made up in another. D ie young and you dodged the aches and pains of growing old, the failing of natural attributes, and the growing inad-

eq uacy. D ie old and you gained the ex tra joys ᴏ
youth.

Why was he thinking about dying when work
waited to be done?

Turning, he looked around. Nyat Cheng was
way over towards the base. A pparently, he'd giv-
en up and was saving further argument until they
had finished their stint. A couple of others were in
view, both hard at work. Ellman aimed his drill,
leaned on it, tripped the mechanism. Chips of rock
flew from beneath the point, deepening the hole
from which he'd removed the scanner. It was
oddly eroded, the lens scarred, the metal sur-
round looking as if it had been abraded with
something like an emery-blast. The replacement
would be set deeper with a new, wide-angle lens,
fitted with a removable cover of transparent plastic.

Setting aside the drill, Ellman crouched,
fighting a sudden giddiness. H e was an electronics
man and a good one. Testing his work was a
waste of time. Each connection was firm, every
terminal correct, and when he did a layout everything was as it should be. To him it was a matter
of pride that it was.

A small thing, perhaps, but important to both
himself and to Alpha.

Now he swore, as his gloved hands were slow
to obey his mental commands. The wires fell,
were recovered, failed to click home. H e paused,
sq ueez ing shut his eyes before trying again. H
was tired, a double shift was enough to take it out

of a giant, but working was better than waiting and if he could do nothing else, he could work.

"G et in!" he muttered. "D amn you, get in!" A gain the wires slipped. There was too little slack, the junctions were awkwardly placed, the connections too tight, the design a lousy combination of some nut-dreamer and a moronic engineer. Why the hell couldn't they build stuff a man could use? "G et in! In!"

H e sighed with relief as the terminals clicked home. A tug to test, a check for fit and the scanner was back in its hold, aligned on its guides, ready to operate as it should.

Chalk up one more success.

H is head reeled as he climbed to his feet, the L unar plain turning, twisting, and heaving as if with a life of its own.

"Tony!" Cheng had been watching. H e began to run as the distant figure swayed. "Move in, Ivan. Fast!"

"G ot it, Nyat." Ivan Cernik lunged forward as fast as safety would allow. H e was close when Ellman began to fall, closer when he spun, to topple, to land with a horrible gasping.

The more horrible sound of escaping air.

"H is faceplate!" H e reached the fallen man, one hand tearing at the emergency patches attached to his thigh, ripping free the adhesive-backed plastic and holding ready as he turned the limp figure. H is guess had been wrong, the helmet was intact, the rupture at a point close to the junction with the suit. A jagged shard of rock had ripped through the tough material.

"Q uick!" Cheng had joined him. "The patch, man! The patch!"

The air-hiss died as it was slapped home, but the horror remained.

"H is face!" Cernik swallowed as he looked at it. "H is face, Cheng! L ook at his face!"

A ge can bring beauty, but only when it is the natural achievement of the passage of time. A wall, mellowed, graced with lichens, hard lines and edges worn and smoothed beneath the hand of years. A garden, grown in harmony, each plant settled in an area hard-won and now its own, colors blending, leaves inter-wound, a whole where there had once been only parts. Those parts now blended and matured with the passing of numerous seasons. Such things held beauty but age, gained without reason, was something else.

H elena R ussell stared at horror.

A horror implied, not actual, for there was nothing really horrible about a face which had grown the deep lines and creped skin of advancing years. Nothing dreadful at seeing the natural state of all living things, providing they manage to survive long enough. No doctor could ever find the relentless workings of catabolism strange and fearful. Men were born, they lived, they grew old, they died. It was the way of the human race.

The horror lay in the unusual.

Tony Ellman was thirty-two years of age.

Now he looked eighty.

H e was eighty.

Mathias was in no doubt.

"Every test proves it, D octor. Blood, marrow, hormones, lymphatic fluids—the man is senile."

"H ow?" Then, as he made no answer, she asked again, more savagely this time, "H ow did it happen? H ow?"

"I don't know."

"But—"

"You asked how it happened and I gave you a truthful reply. I don't know how it happened, but I do know it is an ex tensionof previous discoveries. A ccelerated aging, D octor, a speeded breakdown in the metabolism which leads to inevitable senility." H e added q uietly, "You saw the results of my tests. You made checks yourself. What we suspected then is now a fact."

O ne she wasreluctant to accept, and still q uestions remained ones which could be answered.

"Ellman was a patient together with G reg Sanderson. H e was under observation for strained ligaments and a cartilage operation on the knee. H ealing was slow, but not ex tremelyslow."

"A s it was with Sanderson," Mathias admitted. "A connection?"

"Both were outside workers. Both could have been ex posed to an area of intensive radiation of some kind. I'm guessing," she confessed. "No radiation should cause such results—superficial injury, cellular breakdown, cancer, eventual death, yes—but senility?"

"Senility is the breakdown of all normal physical functions coupled with mental aberration," Mathias reminded. "A deranged mind could contribute to the result by failure to maintain control over the bodily processes. Ex posure to radiation could easily cause cortical degeneration."

"A nd eventual physical breakdown," said H elena. "But the time element, Bob? This man aged in a matter of hours. H e was apparently fit when he commenced his duty shift and yet, when found, he was in the last stages of ex haustion. H e was suited, isolated and yet, somehow, he aged fifty years."

A nd was still aging. H elena glanced at the monitors, then through the transparent partition to where Tony Ellman lay in the intensive care unit. The lighting was dim, rich in ultraviolet, the blueish glow giving his skin the wax en appearance of a corpse. H is cheeks were sunken, closed eyes resting in bruised sockets, folds of skin hanging from his jowls. H is hands, thin and fragile, rested on his lap. The bulk of the life-support apparatus covering his torso hid any motion of his chest, and only the winking tell-tales showed that he was still alive.

"H e's going to die, Bob," she said bleakly. "There's nothing we can do to save him."

A patient lost, and one who would not be allowed to rest in peace. D ead he could still talk, with his tissues, glands, bones and brain. With scraps of internal organs, ligaments, sinews, membranes, skin. Items which would be taken and tested and wrung for information. The last service to A lpha Tony Ellman would ever make.

Mathias said thoughtfully, "H e was prone-it has to be the ex planation. Triggered and primed by his earlier ex posure. Then, when he went outside, he was ready to go. The double shift did it and, once started, the aging process was geometrical."

Two becoming four becoming eight becoming six teen becoming thirtytwo—how long would it take for enough cells to die for senility to become obvious? A ll too soon, she thought. O nce started the process would rage through normal tissues like fire through a cornfield ready for harvest. H elena lifted her commlock from her belt. "G et me the Commander." A moment, then, as Koenig's face appeared on the screen, she said, "This is urgent, John. I have to see you."

"Can't it wait?"

"No." H is face and tone betrayed the tension he was under. "No," she said again. "It can't wait."

"Join me in my office in ten minutes." Then, before breaking the connection, he added, "What is it about?"

"U s, John. A ll of us on lpha-we are all facing premature death!"

"A ge!" V ictor Bergman lifted his hands and looked at them. Broad, capable, the backs marked with brown splotches, the knuckles prominent, the nails neatly filed and polished. "There's no doubt, H elena?"

"None." Her eyes moved from Bergman's hands to Koenig's eyes. "Ellman died just after I called you and Bob's doing the autopsy at this moment, but we know what he will find. D eath caused by senescence—I won't bother you with the medical jargon. Just say that he died of old age."

"H e was a young man."

"*Was*, John." She emphasiz ed the past tense. "But not now. Something outside drained the life from his body as if he were water and it a sponge." She caught his change of ex pression. "John?"

"Nothing." H e saw her determination and shrugged. "It was just the analogy you used— water and a sponge. I've used it myself."

"A ge," said Bergman again. H e lowered his hands. "A sudden acceleration in the metabolic breakdown, H elena. A m I correct?"

"Yes."

"Caused by some ex ternal force?"

She nodded, sensing there was more to the q uestion, something which, as yet, she didn't understand.

Bergman said q uietly, "It fits the pattern, John. L ife is a form of energy and one more subject to destruction than most. Ellman was somehow more sensitive than the rest. H is insistence on working the double shift was symptomatic of his condition—a sudden and final blaz e of energy similar to the glow of a fire fanned by a wind, brightening before the last of its fuel is ex hausted. H ow long do we have, Hena?"

H e was the oldest and would have the greater personal concern and H elena remembered the way he had lifted his hands as if to study them. A natural reaction—what man could tamely ignore the approach of ex tinction? It was hard not to be able to give comfort.

"I don't know as yet, V ictor, but it can't be long. We were still running tests when Ellman collapsed and had determined that there was a general attrition of the metabolism giving a preponderance to the catabolic factors. Ellman aged fifty years in a matter of hours so, obviously, there must be a collapse point. It is probably a variable governed by the individual resistance of each individual—but all will be affected."

Koenig said, "Is there anything we can do? Some-protection we can adopt?"

"A ll can suggest is that none of those working with Ellman be permitted to leave the shelter of base. They should be found work in the lowest levels. In fact, it would be best if everyone were to be kept deep beneath the rock. It might help."

"I doubt it." Koenig told her of the mysterious beam and energy loss. "The same analogy, H elena—water and a sponge. We're the water and the O mphalos is the sponge. Now it seems it wants to suck up more than we can afford to give. Could there be a connection?"

"Perhaps, but I'll have to make tests to be sure. Cultures could be set and ex posed and checks made to see how the bacteria progress. But, John, can't we use the defense shield? Won't it protect us?"

U sing it would cost energy, but at least it might buy them time. Koenig rose and led the way into Main Mission.

"U pper register, Paul. L et's see that beam." H heard H elena inhale as it appeared on the screens, lambent, cold, and hungry. "U p shield!"

A s it rose, shimmering, scintillating with a brilliant coruscation of sparkling energy, Sandra Benes reported from her station.

"Energy loss thirty-nine percent, Commander."

"Boost to the three-q uarters full! Sandra?"

"Fifty-seven percent total loss."

More than half their generated power streaming wastefully into space. Koenig snapped, "Full power, Paul. H old until I give word to lower."

H e blinked as the shield blaz ed with sudden and savage fury, light and brilliance turning the connecting beam into a glowing cone, solidifying it as dust would a beam of light.

"Commander!"

The internal lights dimmed as Morrow gave the warning. A n alarm sounded, another, warnings that the base was dying, the power which was its life drained from the machines essential to survival. "Commander! You must—"

"Cut!" Koenig anticipated the demand. "Sandra?"

"Power restored. L oss now registering at twenty-two percent."

H igher than before and it would mount. Time was against them in more ways than one. Trapped, dying, their energy draining away—how long could they last?

ni ne

In the darkness something moved, a bulky shape which reflected glitters, the helmet staring with its single eye, dust rising from beneath the boots. A lan Carter watched it, noting how the beam of D ale's light caught the hanging webs and turned them into fairy-shimmers of gossamer rainbows. Sparkling curtains blotched with the suspended dead which hung like dried fruit on the fronds of some alien plant.

L ike flies caught and drained and left as desiccated husks by some monstrous spider.

A n unpleasant analogy and one tooclose to the truth. There was no spider and this chamber was no lair. The dead had not been drained by slavering fangs. The darkness held no alien peril.

But death, when it came, would be just as real.

Irritably Carter shook his head and, rising from where he sq uatted, waited for D ale to join him. For a moment he fumbled. Then the connection snapped into place and they could talk again.

"A nything?"

"No." D ale was curt. "I moved all around the edge of the floor—it was solid all the way. L ots of dust and some box es. A litter of fragments which could have been anything. I didn't waste time ex amining them."

"No traps?"

"I told you—nothing." O ver the direct link Carter could hear the man take a deep breath, and when he nex t spoke his voice held a forced lightness. "Well, Skipper, I guess this is it, right?"

"Wrong."

"You're an optimist. The door's sealed, the chamber is solid, and the radios don't work so we can't call for help — are you hoping for a miracle?"

"We're not dead yet," said Carter. "A nd while there's life—"

"—there's hope." D ale finished the q uotation. "They used to teach me that at Sunday School but I never managed to figure out just what it meant. H ope for what? Me, I'd settle for a radio that worked, or a mining drill which could drill a way out of here, or a rescue party suddenly appearing right in front of us. H ope!" H is voice carried resignation. "Maybe we should just sit down and pray?"

Carter said flatly, "I've done that. Now let's take another look at that door."

It was as they had left it, a metal slab firmly set in the octagonal jamb. The inner wheel bore the same ring of symbols, but no matter how he turned it, Carter hadn't been able to swing it free. Now he tried again, trying to remember the ex act seq uence he had used before. A double wiggle like a twisted helix , an interwound line, a pattern of superimposed stars. The door stayed sealed.

"Something must have closed it," said D ale. "But what?"

"We know what closed it." Carter turned the knurled wheel, trying again. With three symbols there would have been six possible combinations. The marked ring held fifteen—it could take a thousand years to hit the correct seq uence by trial and error. "We felt the shift of the floor. The planetoid must have tilted a little on its ax is."

O nly a little, but it would have been enough to swing shut the counterbalanced door. To turn the chamber of the dead aliens into a human tomb.

"L et me try," said D ale as Carter dropped his hands from the wheel. "Maybe I can hit it."

"Keep trying," said Carter. "I'm going to take a look around."

H e jerked free the connecting wire and let it wind back on its spring-loaded spool. Now the silence within his helmet was broken only by the sound of his own breathing, the gentle susurration of circulating air. Normally the sound was almost inaudible, noticed only when absent. Now it had grown to dominate all others.

When it ceased, he would die.

A matter neither of them had mentioned because each knew it too well. D eath waited, not in the alien chamber, but in their own air tanks. It grew as the ox ygen diminished, would strike when the last dregs had been used, would claim its own when, asphyx iated, they succumbed to the final, eternal darkness.

H e stumbled and almost fell, regaining his balance to look down to where a tangle of metal rods lay at his feet. Stooping, he picked them up, turning them, studying their arrangement. L oops and eyes and interlocking bars forming a peculiar combination of unknown purpose. A toy? A n instrument of some kind? A religious object? D iscarded junk? H ow to read an alien mind?

Carter moved on, turning once to look at D ale where he stood before the door, reflected light haloing helmet and suit and turning him into a biz arre presentation of the human shape.

The juncture of the walls and floor was, he knew, solid. Previous investigations had shown the floor to be the same. H igher, beyond reach, darkness ran from the moving circle of his light, the webs casting lacey shadows, colors sparkling to fade and die, to return with swaths of somber hue.

Webs which had to be suspended from something. The rods he had found perhaps?

Carter knelt, rolled on to his back, stared upwards towards the roof as he inched himself across the dust. A race which used webs as couches could have had an avian ancestry— certainly they would have had little fear of heights. L iving in a practically threedimensional area, they would have placed doors and entrances without regard to the factors which guided human use. Perhaps beyond the range of his vision another opening could be found.

Dale turned as Carter slapped his hand on the other's helmet. O nce connected, he said, "No luck, Skipper. The wheel just turns and turns. I've tried until I'm diz z y."

"Sit down. R est a while. Step up the ox ygen."

They had cut down the flow to conserve supplies but had paid for it with rapid fatigue and a slowness of mental aptitude. Now as they sq uatted, Carter opened his valve and watched as D ale did the same.

"H ow long, Skipper?"

H e was talking about their life ex pectancy but Carter deliberately misunderstood.

"Not long. Torens knows we went down the shaft. H e knows we've broken communication. H e'll come looking for us."

"A nd find what?" D ale snorted. "There's a maz e outside that door, so how can he trail us? A nd even if he could, how can he know we're behind that door? A nd even if he does know, how can he open it?"

"The trouble with you," said Carter, "is that you're a pessimist. L ook on the bright side. We are alive, we have air, we have our brains and we have help coming from outside. It's just a matter of time."

"So why am I worried?"

"I told you, it's because you're a pessimist. A n optimist now, well, he would say that we've a nice, snug place to sit in, interesting things to see, a little problem to solve and so ex ercise our brains, and a story to tell our grandchildren."

"Skipper, you're a fool," said D ale, but his tone was lighter than it had been. The graveyard humor had worked—for this time at least, but Carter knew that it wouldn't continue to dispel the inevitable fear and depression the future would bring. The panic too, perhaps the one thing above all they had to guard against.

H e said, "D ale, I've been thinking. These people must have come in here for safety. The door was scaled—so why there isn't any air?"

For a moment the co-pilot remained silent, then he grunted. "No air? O f course! Why didn't I think of that?"

"Think of it now," urged Carter. It would be better if D ale could provide the answers. "No air why?"

"It could have leaked. This place is old and over the years it could have seeped away."

"Possible," admitted Carter, "but this chamber is lined with the same olive metal as the shaft and tunnels. A s far as we can see it's intact. A nd look at the dust, if there had been a trace of air when we opened the door it would have blown towards us. It didn't."

"So this place was a vacuum when we found it." D ale was thoughtful. "A fissure maybe? A crack leading outside?"

"That or another door—an open door."

"A way out!" D ale sucked in his breath. "Skipper, you're a genius. Now tell me where it's to be found."

"U p," said Carter. "Somewhere up high. It has to be."

In the mirror the face was smooth, the skin clear, marked only by the thin lines of character, the mold of muscle and bone? H ow long would it be before age marred the contours, sagged the flesh, turned the present features into a raddled mask?

Thinking of it, H elena R ussell lifted a hand and touched the mane of golden hair, soon to turn white, to grow brittle, to hang in stringy tufts from the dome of her scalp. To grow old was nothing given the time to do it. But if she, suddenly, became a thing of senility and decay...

The hum of her commlock broke the train of thought and she lifted the instrument from her belt, glad of the interruption, the electronic contact with others of her kind.

Koenig looked at her from the screen. H e was worried.

"H elena, some trouble. A lan and his pilot are missing. A t least they are out of contact."

"Missing?" She remembered the mission he had led. "O n the planetoid?"

"H e found a shaft of some kind and investigated it. R adio contact was lost. Torens waited and then landed to search. H e found a maz e of tunnels."

"A nd A lan?"

"No sign of either him or D ale. They might be in need of emergency medical assistance. If you would ask Bob—"

"No," she interrupted. "There's no need for that. I'll meet you on the launching pad in five minutes."

"H elena—"

"D on't waste time arguing, John. Five minutes."

Bergman was seated in the passenger module when she arrived. H e saw her ex pression and guessed what was in her mind.

"No one can live forever, H elena."

"But this is stupid, V ictor. You aren't needed. You should be staying in the lowest depths of A lpha."

"Where I'd be safe?" H e smiled as she made no answer. "A nd what about you?"

"I'm a doctor. It's my job."

"It could be mine. Torens reported a strange olive-colored, metallic-seeming coating lining the shaft and tunnels. It appears to have been placed by an intelligent race. I want to see it, to ex amine it and learn what I can. A s we can't bring the planetoid to me, then I must go to the planetoid." H e grunted as the Eagle lifted, Koenig at the controls. "A nd don't worry about my health. I think that the aging process is a direct result of the beam impinging on the Moon from the O mphalos. We'll be away from it within seconds."

A comfort—why had she been so terrified of sudden age? A n instinctive rejection of the lost opportunities? A nger at the years lost and never lived? V anity?

She thought of Koenig and tried to imagine his face seamed and lined and creped as Ellman's had been. H is shoulders stooped, his limbs wasted, his bones grown brittle, his sharp intellect reduced to senseless wanderings.

It would come. G iven time it would come—why did life have to be so short?

Bergman shrugged as she put the q uestion. "H elena, for some men eternity isn't long enough, and for others a decade is too long. Who can tell? Personally, I hope to live long enough to see the A lphans settled on a new world. O nce that has been accomplished, well, we all have to go, and for me that will be as good a time as any."

To find a new Earth—the hope and dream of them all. To find a world on which they could settle and build and be safe from the perils which menaced them in space. But perhaps they had already left it too late. The doom they had escaped in the past now waited for them here in this alien space. A death from which there seemed to be no escape.

D epressed, she leaned back as the Eagle hurtled through space. From the pilot's seat Koenig said, "Better check your eq uipment, H elena. Minutes could count."

H is voice was flat, emotionless, but she could guess his concern.

"It's been done, John. When do we land?"

"Soon." The throb of the engines at full power underlined his terseness. "Torens will be waiting."

H e stood, suited, his copilot beside him on the smooth ex panse of the planetoid. Carter's Eagle was to his rear, the open hole of the shaft at his feet. H e gestured towards it as Koenig and the others came towards him.

"This is it, Commander. I've scanned the area and found no other opening. If they came out at all it had to be from here."

"A nd they didn't?"

"No." Torens was positive. "I've been operating a continuous scan."

"A nd?"

"I warned A ndrews and went after them. A s I reported, there's a maz e down there. The tunnels are lined with metal of some kind which seems to act as a radio-barrier." The man realiz ed he was repeating himself, wasting time relaying information which they already knew. "Your orders?"

"We go down. Signal A ndrews to hover low and maintain general watch." Koenig forced himself to contain his impatience. "Then follow us down. But waste no time."

H urry before the store of air was ex hausted and the need for rescue had passed. Before the men died from lack of ox ygen and the base had lost two good workers. Before he lost an old and valued friend.

Bergman grunted as he landed at the foot of the shaft. Metal glinted in his hand as he scratched at the olive surface.

"This coloring is like a patina, John. Similar to that found on bronz e. Beneath the metal is incredibly hard and dense. It would be interesting to discover how it was worked."

"L ater." Koenig was following Torens's cepilot along the passage. "H elena, stay close."

She came after him, her medical bag slung over her shoulder, Koenig carrying the more bulky eq uipment, the sac which couldbe sealed around the doctor and her patient inflated, to permit her to remove a suit and give emergency treatment if necessary.

"We left a trail," ex plained Jackson, the ce pilot. "See?" H e pointed to a thin line of white powder which lay on the floor. "A **d** we left other marks on the walls ahead. If you want to keep in touch, you'd better make wire-connections now."

A few moments and it was done, Koenig thinning his lips at the essential delay.

"D id you find anything other than passages? Traps, alcoves, chambers?"

"No, Commander."

"A ny upwardeading shafts?"

"No." Jackson grunted as he bumped into a wall. "Nothing."

A n answer which made no sense. Men couldn't simply vanish without cause. The corridors seemed solid, the floor, the roof. The tunnels, branching and forking, formed an intricate maz e, but with the white powder tracing their path and marks on the walls, they were covering every foot.

ROGUE PLANET

Koenig halted as he saw whiteness in the beam of his fight.

"We've covered this part."

"There's another passage to the right," said Bergman. H e headed towards it, the connecting wire growing taut, slackening as he halted. "We've covered that too. John, there has to be something we haven't spotted as yet. A room in which they are trapped, maybe. A chute down which they have fallen. They could be inches from us. O n the other side of a wall."

But without a means of communication they would never know.

A nd both air and time were running out.

D ale sagged, the sound of his breathing harsh, ragged, a wheez e in his throat andlungs. "No," he said. "D amn it, Skipper, no. There isn't a door. There isn't even a hole large enough to pass a cat. You were wrong."

Wrong, thought Carter bleakly, but not wholly so. H e looked at the thin crack in the circle of light thrown by his helmet, the only flaw in the walls and roof they had found. A small thing, barely noticeable, one they would not have discovered at all, if it hadn't been for the five bodies lying beneath it, the clutter of inter-wound rods.

A ladder the dead had tried to use in a final attempt to seal the crack.

O ne which had bled the air from the chamber in a slow but relentless harbinger of death.

H is boot hit a heap of dust as he turned and led the way back towards the door. G rit flew and something hard rolled to settle a few feet ahead. Stooping he picked it up and rolled it in his gloved hand. A stone, elaborately carved, set in a curved band of metal. A bracelet or an arm band. A n item of jewelry once priz ed and now less than rubbish.

Carter slipped it over his forearm, the metal hitting the power-pack on his chest unit as he lowered his hand, a sharp click sounding in his helmet.

D ale said, "What was that, Skipper?"

"What?"

"A click. I heard it through my phones."

"You did?" Carter frowned, trying to think and finding it difficult. The air, he knew, was too vitiated, too rich in waste and too low in ox ygen. The result of deliberately adjusting the valves. Ex tra life had been gained at the ex pense of mental alertness.

"A click." D ale was insistent. To him in his low condition it had become a very important problem to be painstakingly solved. "In my phones. In my phones, Skipper."

Carter looked down at his chest unit. The power pack's indicator glowed, the batteries at almost full charge. H e hit it again with the metal band and then, with sudden clarity, was jerking at the catches.

"Skipper?" D ale caught at his arm. "You craz y or something?"

"No."

"Then—"

"They're out there looking for us, right? The Commander," he yelled as D ale made no answer. "Torens and the others. They can't be far, but they can't hear us. We've no radio."

"So?"

"We'll make noise. They must be using direct commlinks if they're in the tunnels. Now listen." H e touched the band to the battery terminals, creating an arc, a minute flare which caused a crackle in his earphones. "O ld fashioned radio," he said. "A spark gap. They can't pick it up on U H, but it might trigger their phones. A ll we need is to create noise." H e manipulated the band, concentrating on his fingers the sounds which buz z ed from his phones. Three shorts, three longs, three shorts. S.O .S. The old call for help in a code developed long before he'd been born. "G et it, D ale?"

"I get it." The man slumped against the door. H is voice was tired, slurred. "Morse Code. Can I help, Skipper? Can I—"

"You can sit, save your breath and hang on. A nd," Carter added grimly, "you can pray some-one hears us."

A prayer that was answered.

Koenig frowned as his phones buz z ed, the sound repeated to form a pattern.

"John!" H elena turned to face him. "What?"

"Silence!" H e held up one hand. "A ll of you, be q uiet and listen." H e held his breath as the buz z ing continued. "It's code."

"A call for help, John." Bergman threw his light against the walls around them. "From the missing men, obviously, but where are they?"

"A door," snapped Koenig. "L ook for a door."

H elena found it, spotting the thin lines depicting the octagonal opening, catching the outline in a shift of the light. Koenig dropped to his knees and lowered his helmet to the floor. Staring over the surface, he saw little scuffs in the fine tracery of dust.

"This is it. V ictor, how can we get it open?"

Bergman said dubiously, "I'm not sure, John. We'll need lasers and drills at least. If we try to blow it open, we could kill the others. If we could only talk to them, perhaps they could tell us how they got inside."

Jackson had brought a heavy crowbar with him. Koenig took it, lifted it, sent it smashing hard against the door. Three times he repeated the blows, then paused. The impact would be unheard unless one or the other was in direct contact with the metal, but the chance was worth taking. A fter a moment he repeated the blows, paused, slammed at the metal-again.

Inside the chamber D ale stirred and said, "Skipper, my head. I keep getting sounds in my head."

"Clicks?"

ROGUE PLANET

"No." Clumsily D ale moved, his suited figure rolling away from the door against which he had been leaning. "Thuds like a hammer was at work. A hammer," he muttered and then suddenly retched. "A ir—I've gotta have air!"

H e was dying. H ad he been deep water he would have inhaled his lungs full of liq uid, compelled by the sheer necessity to breathe, a reflex over which he would no longer have control. A s it was, in the suit, he could do nothing but gasp and flounder like a landed fish, inhaling stale poison, trying to rid himself of it, in danger of strangling on his own vomit.

Kneeling, Carter spun the valves, flushing out the air cylinder and feeding the last puff of precious ox ygen to the helpless man.

Without air the man would die, and q uickly. Carter, without hesitation, connected a feed line from his own ox ygen supply to D ale's and began to supply him with part of his remaining supply. H e intended to share half of his air, but as he neared the cutoff point, he became lightheaded, fumbled at the control knob and the halfway mark was passed before he stopped it. It was impossible to do anything about it. H is supply was nearly ex hausted; only a difference in metabolism had enabled him to last a little longer. H e hoped his actions and his constitution would allow both of them to survive until their rescuers arrived. Tiredly he leaned back against the door, the crude signals forgotten as he rested his helmet against the metal.

A nd heard the repeated thud of blows.

The band slipped in his fingers, almost fell, lifted as if it weighed a ton to touch the terminals and to flash its spark and electronic noise. Not to call for help—that had arrived—but to relay the most important information of all.

"D oor... wheel... combo lock," his finge spelled out the words. "Wriggle... coil... stars. Se q uence... helix ... twist... stars. D oor... w lock... hurry!"

The thud of blows signaling what? A greement, understanding, mystification? H ad they heard at all? Could they hear? Would the door open if they could?

The band fell and he picked it up, darkness edged his vision, the sour taste of acid in his throat, pain growing in his lungs. H e retched, spattering the interior of his helmet with a thin wetness, then retched again, dry heaves which tore at his lungs and sent stars to flame in ruby dartings against the growing darkness. D ying.

H e was dying!

A nd then suddenly there was peace.

t en

H elena said sharply, "The tanks, q uickly!"

Bergman was already at work, kneeling beside one of the sprawled figures, his hands deft as he undid the connection and fitted the new container of air. A twist of the valve and ox ygen gusted into the suit, chilling but carrying with it the essence of life. To one side H elena was doing the same, checking, probing, her fingers searching for signs of life as her eyes checked monitors. "V ictor?"

"Frank is barely alive but responding."

A lan Carter's readings insisted otherwise. H elena was unwilling to accept a machine's declaration of the end of a life—she knew better.

"H elena?"

"The sac," she snapped. "Quickly!"

In such matters she was to be obeyed. Koenig ripped open the emergency pack, opened the frame that supported the thin but tough membrane, and he and Bergman dragged the two astronauts inside. A s they began to ex it, H elena said, "No! V ictor, you sty with him!"

Koenig disconnected his direct commlink and ex ited. H elena pushed through, carrying her medical case and a spare tank of air and knelt beside the two still figures within. Sealing the bag, he twisted the valve of the cylinder, pressure rounding the sac as it filled with air.

Inside H elena set to work.

Koenig stood by the open door, cursing the delay it had caused. A few minutes earlier and both would have been safe. A little faster in solving the crude message—but to regret was useless, time could not be reversed, what had happened was done. Now, A lan Carter's continued ex istence depended on H elena's skills.

Bergman removed D ale's helmet and cleared his breathing pathway, fitting him with a mask now attached to an ox ygen cylinder.

H elena attended to Carter. H is suit had been flushed but Carter hadn't responded. H e was, she decided, medically dead. H is lungs had ceased to work and his heart to beat—unless the flow of blood could be restored to his brain within minutes he would, if he lived at all, be a mental cripple, the lack of ox ygen having caused irremediable damage.

Minutes—how long had it already been?

H e was dead and only she could restore him. The helmet came free and was thrown to one side. Q uickly she wiped the mouth and chin and similarly placed an ox ygen mask over his flaccid lips. Propping it into position she moved to straddle the supine figure and, stiffening her arms, threw her weight against the torso in the region of the heart. The suit hampered her and made it difficult to hit the right spot, but practice had given her skill and the heels of her hands slammed up beneath the ribs as she massaged the heart. She unsealed her helmet, lifting the face-plate, and now she stooped over the still figure. Inflating her chest, she adjusted his head, pinched his nose closed, then parting his lips, pressed her own against them and forced air into the pilot's lungs.

Inhale, blow, release, inhale, blow, release… pumping air into him as if he were a balloon.

The kiss of life and the only chance he had.

A gain, she massaged the heart, again breathed into him, her mouth against his own.

A gain.

A gain.

A s he made no response, she paused and took a hypodermic from her bag. It was loaded with a heavy dose of adrenaline and ready to fire its charge into the blood stream. She triggered it, sending the drug into the great veins of the neck and again thrust her hands against the torso.

A minute gone at least, maybe two.

"A lan! For G od's sake! A lan!"

Carter stirred, moaned a little, sucked air into his lungs. H elena straightened, still straddled across his body, her helmet touching the top of the sac. From her bag she took a phial and sprayed an acrid compound into his mouth and nostrils. H e coughed, choked a little and opened his eyes.

"A lan. D o you know who you are?"

"I—" His eyes rolled a little, vague, empty. "Who? What? You—"

She said again, her voice holding the sting of a whip, "Who are you? Tell me who you are!"

The essential test of identity. He could have been dead too long, the ego already impaired, his personality changed, blurred, distorted. If so, it might have been kinder if she'd let him go. She put the thought out of her mind.

"Alan?"

"Doctor!" His eyes settled, became bright with life and awareness. "Doctor Russell!"

"Who are you? Tell me?" She relaxed as he obeyed, adding other information, proving that his intelligence was unimpaired. "Relax," she ordered as he began to move. "Don't try to move just yet. Just lie and breathe and let your heart and lungs achieve full automatic operation."

"I'm all right, Doctor."

"Yes, thank God!"

Her tone betrayed her and, staring up into her face, Carter said slowly, "It was close, eh? I'd passed out. I remember that I was retching, then seemed to be falling, and then there was nothing. It was odd in a way. As if, at the end, nothing really mattered. That all the struggle and fear were over. And then—" He broke off then added slowly, "I was dead. Dead, and you resurrected me."

Her hand reached for another hypodermic, this one loaded with a tranquilizer. She had won the battle with death before and knew what could so easily happen. The resurgence of life, the euphoria, the biological reaction which affected men and women alike and was the most common cause of romantic associations formed by patients for their doctors and nurses.

Carter saw the instrument in her lifted hand and said dryly, "You know, D octor, this is getting to be a habit. If it keeps up, I'll be so compromised that you'll have to marry me."

A joke and his way of telling her that the danger she feared did not ex ist, that he needed no chemical help to regain his normal emotional eq uilibrium.

Then, as she restored the hypodermic to her bag, he said, "I was lucky. You got to me in time. But D ale? What about D ale?"

"H e's recovering. H e'd passed out before you did. That may have saved his life."

Koenig watched H elena and her patients leave, carried in Torens's Eagle. Carter had sworn that he was fit for duty, but Koenig had insisted, and he'd had no choice but to obey.

A s the Eagle dwindled and vanished from sight he turned to where Bergman was kneeling, his gloved hands probing at the ground.

"H ave you noticed anything strange about this place, John?"

"It's small and round and apparently smooth," said Koenig and added dryly, "I've been a little too busy to pay much attention to the scenery."

"The chamber." Bergman rose. "A nd that metal lining the tunnels. The inscriptions too, all most interesting."

A nd food for later study if ever they had the time or opportunity. A lready A ndrews's pilot had taken a series of photographs and was even now attempting to remove a segment of the stuff from the rim of the shaft. H e was finding it hard work.

"A t first ex amination it looks as if at one time it was a mine," said Bergman. "But I don't think it could have been that. Maybe, at first, but certainly not for some time. The galleries, if any ex isted, have all been sealed and that chamber with the bodies—most unusual." H e moved his boot over the soil, scraping at the dirt with its edge. It rose in a mound of fine particles to form a heap resembling ash.

"The inner lock of the door was broken," Bergman mused. "It must have been done deliberately which means that the creatures who sealed themselves in the chamber had no intention of ever leaving it. Perhaps they couldn't. Perhaps there was nowhere else they could go." A gain, his boot scraped at the gritty soil. "A last stand," he said thoughtfully. "The final retreat. D id they continue to hope, I wonder? D id some take their own lives? O r did they wait until their air escaped and died as they had lived, in a common unity?"

"If they had lived that way."

"They could live in no other, John. It took co-operation to work that metal, to form it, to set it into place. It took more to arrive at a common decision and to stick to it. To fashion the chamber and to enter it and wait. Perhaps they still had hope, John, but I doubt it. They would have seen too much, ex perienced too crushing a defeat for hope to have remained. A nd yet they must have had determination." H e paused then said wistflly, "I wish that we could have known them. There would have been much we could have learned, and towards the end, at least, we'd have had much in common."

The mutual necessity which had driven them to burrow deep into the ground, to construct tunnels, chambers, a means to survive. In that, at least, the aliens and the A lphans were alike. A common need and a common enemy. A common death, perhaps.

Koenig said, "The beam?"

"It's obvious what it does, John. This is the final proof if we should need it. A force which weakens the molecular and atomic bonds and attracts the latent energy of matter itself. This planetoid could have been much larger than it is now. In fact, I'm certain of it.

"The bodies we found prove that. There could have been an atmosphere, water, soil, growing things, villages even. A small world but a pleasant one. Then it entered this space—or perhaps, more likely, this pocket of space passed through a planetary system and its path intersected with this world—and it was trapped by the O mphalos It's all relative... "

Caught to be eaten by the beam, as a boy would gnaw at an apple on a stick. Matter reduced to energy and drawn away and, as the balance was altered, the tiny world would have turned to ex pose a fresh portion of its surface to the devouring energy. Such a minute shift must have caused the closing of the door which had trapped Carter and D ale. Koenig said, "H ow fast, V ictor?"

"D oes the beam convert matter into energy? I don't know, John, we'll have to make tests to find out. But I don't think that it can be very fast. If the energy is liberated too q uickly it could overload whatever mechanism or function the O mphalos uses to absorb it. A nd the people here had time to construct their tunnels."

D igging like desperate rats to escape the inevitable. D elving deeper and deeper into their world as the surface was stripped away. Fighting to obtain a defense against premature aging, waiting, hoping, breeding, dying until, at the end, there was no more hope, nothing but ex tinction.

H ow long would it be until the A lphans reached that point?

H ow many generations? H ow many millennia? A ges? Eons?

A nd if they followed the same path would the final victims be even human? "John?"

"I was thinking, V ictor."

"O f A lpha." Bergman was shrewd. "I know. The pattern is similar."

The pattern, perhaps, but not necessarily the ingredients. The A lphans were human with all that implied. Born and reared against a background of ceaseless effort, their lives a continual act of violence, they had survived only because their planet had known they were the most ruthless of all life-forms.

O beying a simple, savage creed.

To kill what they feared.

To destroy all that threatened.

Koenig said, "V ictor, when you've finished here return to base in A ndrews's Eagle."

"A nd you, John?"

"I'm going to visit the O mphalos."

H e traveled alone, if death waited there was no point in sharing the burden. The Eagle rose, leaving the planetoid behind as the engines sent it across space towards the pulsating green mass of the O mphalos. Koenig avided the energy-beam, swinging around until he was at a point between the Moon and the remnant of what had once been an inhabited world, then aimed the nose of the Eagle at its target.

"Commander?" Morrow stared from the screen. H e blinked as Koenig gave is orders. "A relay from Main Mission on upper register? Sure. I'll put it on the secondary channel. Two minutes."

It appeared in one, the O mphalos a pale violet, the energy beams clear. Koenig looked at the image, comparing it with the direct view. O n the relay his Eagle would be visible if Morrow increased the magnification, but he could do that only by narrowing the area of the visible field. It was better to scan a wider area—Koenig knew where he was.

"Commander?" Morrow was concerned. "You're going in alone—how about some support?"

"No."

"I could send more Eagles for rescue and as a backup and—"

"No, Paul!" Koenig snapped his impatience. "I'm doing this alone. Watch and monitor but no support and no interference. Maintain continual check on all energy fluctuations. A ctivate defense shield at low power and try to hit a bearable compromise between protection and power loss. U n-derstood?"

"Yes, Commander."

"I'm making a reconnaissance," said Koenig, more softly. "Just a general probe to gather readings at close prox imity. V ictor should be with you soon but, until he arrives, you are in full command."

H e broke the connection; there was nothing more to say, nothing more to do now but wait, as the engines killed the distance between the Eagle and its destination. Time to relax in the padded chair, to think, to speculate a little.

A brain.

H elena's analogy had been good and the likeness persisted, even though he was seeing it from
a different angle and from a closer point. The
convoluted surface, the dark lines, the division
between the hemispheres—all backed the similarity. But no brain could live without a body, a
source of energy to maintain it, a skull to protect
it. The thing could only be a mass of ordinary
matter, barren, lifeless.

But, in that case, why did it pulsate?

A n illusion? A trick of the light deceiving the
eyes? Koenig narrowed his own watching, timing
the apparent swell. R eal or imagined? A thickening of the haz e followed by a clarity would produce such a result. A gentle inflation and deflation
the same. Even a steady rippling of the surface—
but how could a solid mass ripple in such a manner?

H e glanced at the upper register. The pale violet of the image was steadier than the normal
view in green. The twin cones of pale luminescence seemed to drift over the surface as they
followed the orbiting masses of the Moon and the
planetoid.

L ike hands, he thought, ex tended and grasp-
ing. L ike the antennae of insects, the feelers of
things which lived in darkness, the suckers of an
octopod.

Koenig shook his head, irritated at his fantasies. H e studied his instruments, seeing that the
temperature of the O mphalos was still apparently

z ero despite the energy intake and its luminescence.

Well, soon now he might have the answer.

"Commander—you're getting close."

Morrow on the screen with a warning Koenig could do without. H e acknowledged it with a grunt, then concentrated on sending the Eagle into a spiraling orbit around the pulsating central mass of this pocket universe.

Closer and he could see the convolutions, now stark and clear. Not deep valleys as he had ex - pected, but gashes dulled with ebon tracery lying somber and menacing in the twinkling haz e. Closer still and beneath him, the alien landscape spun towards the rear in a blur of mounds, dells, scoops, peaks, twistings, blurs, spinnings, whirlings, swirlings... windings... writhings.

Confusion which rose to engulf him. "Koenig! John Koenig! You will hear me and you will obey!"

A voice echoing in his mind, reverberating, booming as if from the far end of a long tunnel, amplified and empty, a remnant of the past.

"John Koenig, you will succumb to my will. You are helpless to resist. You will obey... obey... obey... "

A schoolyard, a gang, an older boy confident of his physical strength, the loyalty of his buddies. A spiritual weakling, a sadist, a vicious bully.

"John Koenig, you will obey me without q ues- tion. You will obey me in all things. You will obey!"

Now, as he had then, Koenig shouted his defiance.

"G o to hell!"

"What? You—"

"G o to hell!"

The voice was an illusion, a revived scrap of memory triggered by the hypnotic condition of the greenish illumination. It had to be that. R ock and stone and raw energy were not alive. Nothing could be alive in this seething hell.

Nothing—then why did he see a smirking face?

Pain stung the inside of his lip as his teeth met in the tender flesh. A stab of agony which cleared his eyes and banished the confusion, so that he could clearly see the shape and position of the instruments before him, the controls of the Eagle in which he rode.

A switch which he closed.

"Paul!" he gasped. "Paul, help me... help... "

A moment of clarity, gone almost as q uickly as it had come, replaced by the swirling confusion which rose to take him and hurl him into chaos.

el ev en

H e was a mote of life drifting in an endless, emerald sea. The waters were warm and comforting, lulling him with gentle surges, carrying him over a vast ex panse of fretted stone and shells and strands of delicate weed. O ther life drifted around him, small, innocent scraps of awareness conscious only of the need to eat and to propagate, the sole pleasure of their limited ex istence.

When death came in a darting shadow of fin and jaw it was nothing.

A gain he drifted, this time in an atmosphere of gentle breez es and solemn silences, the sun a shimmering orb of emerald splendor. A gain he was minute, but this time a little larger than before. A thinly constructed creature of vanes and sacs filled with hydrogen, of foils to catch and use the wind, of muscles to bunch and make dense his bodily substance so that, at will, he could gain height or lose it, could drift with the wind or tack against it.

H e and the uncountable numbers of others who hung with him in the emerald sky.

Food for larger beings of more complex structure. D rifting giants who roved the atmosphere and browsed on the clouds of things of which he was a single part.

A nd again, when death came, it was nothing. D eath was always nothing.

The gateway to a new ex istence, a door which all things had to use, a path every living creature had to take. D eath was not an ending but a new beginning. The old cells and structure broken, torn into their component parts, incorporated into other, more sophisticated arrangements. The pattern of the mind released from its fleshy bonds to free the spirit, which would pass on to join the single great accumulation of all feeling, all ex perience, all knowledge, all awareness, a consciousness which was the gestalt of the universe.

A nd it was right that the larger should feed on the smaller, the lesser give its awareness and substance to a thing of greater complex ity. A s atoms had been created in the empty spaces to form molecules and compounds and thus the basic matter of planets and suns, so the single-celled gave to the many-celled and they, in turn, gave to those higher on the evolutionary scale.

The way of life and the arrow of time. The ladder which reached from primeval mud to the stars.

The sacrifice which gave the ultimate peace. Peace.

"No!" Koenig stirred, something within him rebelling, waking, protesting. "No!"

"Such foolishness," whispered a thin voice. "Such stupidity. What are a few days when set against the total span of time? What is a lifetime when set against eternity?"

"No, damn you! No!"

"Why fight, John Koenig? Why continue to carry the burden? You've carried it long enough and there will be no end to the weight, the responsibility, the guilt. You killed Tony Cellini. You killed D an Mateo. You killed Sam and Tessa. You killed... you killed... you killed..."

The list of names seemed endless.

The guilt a burden on his soul.

Each who had died and who would die was his concern. H e was the commander, his, the decision, and therefore his, the responsibility. A lways his was the responsibility. A lways his would be the guilt.

A lways.

"No," he said, stubbornly. "It isn't like that."

"But it is, John Koenig," whispered the voice. "It always has been. It always will be. H ow many can you order to their deaths? H ow long can you rest hearing their cries and reproaches? O ne mistake and all will die. O ne mistake...one... only one... "

O nce dead, he would be freed from the possibility that he would make that mistake.

"No," he said again. "No."

The voice was a lie. It was the sound of cowardice, the lure of timidity. Yield, give up, cease the struggle and be rewarded with eternal rest. A bribe which had no substance.

Who was tempting him?

ROGUE PLANET

Who—or what?

A red eye began to blink at him, flash... flash... flash... A cyclops which demanded attention. Koenig stared at it, seeing it through a green haz e, a swirl of distorted reality. It was hard to concentrate. It would be easier simply to lean back and relax and to close his eyes and to sink into that wonderful state of utter detachment in which nothing had importance and nothing really mattered because, in the end, all things would be the same.

So easy to lean back... to drift... to drift...

Paul Morrow scowled at his instruments, the ex pression accentuating the lines on his face, the fatigue. A deep, bone-nagging weariness aggravated by his frustration.

"Nothing." H e checked a row of instruments, fingers stabbing at buttons, cross-meshing circuits. From the console, little lamps flared, telltales merging with illuminated dials and digital readouts, monitors which told him the condition of every sector of the base. "Nothing," he said again. "The Eagle's dead."

"Keep trying." V ictor Bergman studied the screens, the images they carried. "Keep trying, Paul."

"I'm sending out a continuous signal but there's no answer. I've tried to use the override but there's no response. Something is cancelling out the signals and I can't gain remote control. Try, you say." H is voice rose a little, grew bitter. "D amn it, Professor! D o you think I've just been sitting here twiddling my thumbs?! I've tried everything I know!"

"No, Paul, of course not." Fatigue bred short tempers, but, as Bergman knew, Morrow's outburst was less due to weariness than to a stronger feeling. H e, like all of them, was sick with worry and concern for the lone man in the distant Eagle.

"H e hasn't landed," said Morrow q uietly. "H e orbiting the O mphalos but so close he must be skimming the edge of any force-field it might have. Field or atmosphere," he added bleakly. "G od alone knows what he's found out there."

"Sandra?"

"No change, Professor. I have been monitoring the path of the Commander's flight pattern and there is no discernible energy variation."

"Which means that he can hardly be cutting through a force-field if one should ex ist," mused Bergman. "If he was, we'd surely spot a halation."

"O nly if the situation out there followe d a familiar electronic seq uence." Sandra checked her instruments again. "Surface temperature still z ero. No measurable radiation. No magnetic flux . There seems to be no reason why the Commander cannot just level orbit and head back to A lpha."

"Paul?"

"H is guidance systems could be froz en in some way. I've sent out checking signals and received no response, but that could be due to a different cause." Morrow shook his head, baffled. "H e's out there. We know it and know just where to find him. A s far as I ca determine all systems are operational."

"So?"

"Either the Commander has deliberately cut the remotes, or they have failed to function because of some local effect. The O mphalos could be surrounded with a blanket of electronic distortion which traps all emissions. That could ex plain why I'm getting no personal contact."

"But surely the Commander would know that and return?" Sandra Benes, well-versed in survival disciplines, knew the regular safety procedure. "H e would not risk his life and an Eagle for noting."

Bergman said, "Perhaps he has no choice."

"Professor?"

"H e could be unconscious or hurt in some way. It is the only ex planation for his continued radio silence, unless the O mphalos has a distortion field as Paul suggests. A t this very moment the Commander could be calling on us for help." Bergman frowned at the screens. "Paul, is an energy-cone impinging on the Eagle?"

"No."

A nother mystery why cones on the Moon and the planetoid and not on the Eagle? The mass too small perhaps? The object too near?

Q uestions which could wait but one problem could not.

"Kano, have you checked the rate of descent? H ow much time do we have before the Eagle crashes?"

ROGUE PLANET

From where he stood beside the computer, David Kano said, "What's on your mind, Professor? Rescue?"

"Is it possible?"

Kano fed the problem into the machine and tore the slip from the readout.

Morrow saw him frown. "What's wrong, David?"

"A moment." Again, Kano busied himself with the computer, made a check, looked up from the final result. "A new factor has been added," he said bleakly. "The rate of orbital decay is accelerating faster than it should. Either something has slowed the Eagle or it is being affected by a force from below."

"Well?"

"At the present velocity and with the decay remaining as plotted, we have time to reach the Eagle and have approximately ten minutes in which to effect an exchange and escape."

Ten minutes! It would have to be enough.

Alan Carter sat in the pilot's chair. He had heard the news and had risen from his hospital bed and had insisted on his right to command the rescue ship. A right backed by his unquestioned skill.

"You'll need the best," he'd said. "I'm the best. I've the training and the experience and if I can't do it no one can. Not a boast, Professor, a fact and you know it."

"But are you fit?"

"I'm fit." Carter had shrugged. "So I lost my breath for a while—I've got it back now. I've had plenty of time to regain it and I'll have more on the journey out. D avid can pilot the Eagle until we reach the O mphalos." H e added impatuntly, "L et's not argue about it—we haven't time for that."

But time had been found to install a few items of eq uipment Bergman had selected. Time, too, for H elena R ussell to bring aboard things of her own.

L ike A lan Carter, she had insisted on accompanying the rescue mission and, like Carter, she was not to be denied.

Now she busied herself in the passenger module, mix ing fluids, sealing small containers, fastening them to pipes leading to masks which could be clipped over the mouth and nostrils. Standard eq uipment which Bergman recogniz ed as being parts of emergency resuscitation apparatus.

"H ere, V ictor." She handed him one. "L oop this over your head and hook the container onto your belt. Wear the mask or leave it to rest just below your mouth. There's a valve here, see? Turn it if you feel odd in any way."

"Such as?"

"G iddiness, detachment, disorientation."

"You ex pect such reactions?"

"I don't know what to ex pect, V ictor, but I'm trying to anticipate. John wouldn't just freez e unless he had no choice. The Eagle is protected against most things, and if the trouble is other than physical, what I've built won't help much. The flasks contain an anti-hallucinogen in liq uid form under pressure. Turning the valve will release a fine spray which will turn into a vapor. It will do as much as the capsules I made before we hit this space. If we are subjected to sensory distortion or cerebral stimulation, then the gas could help."

"H ow? A s a depressant?" Bergman was interested. A djusting the device, he twisted the alve and took a cautious sniff. "It smells like ammonia."

"A scent incorporated as a warning that the valve is open," she ex plained. "A lso, it serves to tighten the inner membranes and clear the nasal passages so as to allow an easy entry of the vapor into the lungs. The chemical formula is complex , an ex tension of what I used before." She added somberly, "I hope that it can help."

A s Bergman hoped that his own devices would work.

A s H elena rose to carry other containers of the anti-hallucinogen to where Kano and Carter sat in the pilot's seats of the Eagle, he stooped over the apparatus he had brought with him. It was a jumble of electronic circuits, radiant coils, batteries, resonators, crystals and other assorted pieces of electronic eq uipment snatched from his laboratory. Now he connected parts to each other, fed power into the assembly, watched as dials kicked and registers glowed.

R eturning, H elena watched him, saw his frown, his irritable shake of the head. "Trouble, V ictor?"

"Yes."

"What is it?"

"Something I've been working on. A compact form of a heterodyning apparatus which I intended to fit to the regular screen installations of the Eagles. A s you know, there are two ways at least of gaining protection from energies which may threaten to disrupt or damage life and eq uipment. We can prevent it reaching us—in other words, set up a barrier of some kind which is stronger than the threatening energy—or we can diffuse it. O ur present defense shield works on the former principle. We set up an umbrella of controlled energy, held and directed by powerful fields which are strong enough to prevent the passage of inimical forces. It also helps to diffuse the energy by forcing it to spread its point of impact, so that no one point is subjected to the total."

"L ke a shield of steel fronted by a liter of fluid," she said. "The fluid spreads the impact and the steel stops it. I understand."

"Such a system req uires weight and a plentiful supply of power." Bergman made another adjustment and grunted as a lamp flashed. "I'm trying to do something different."

"H eterodyning," she said. "Cancelling out. O ne force merging with and diminishing another. I remember an ex periment conducted in the science lab when I was at school. Two different sounds which were blended to result in silence. Two lights the same. A s I remember it, the crests of one wave-form had to match ex actly with the valleys of another. By combining the two you ended with a total cancellation of both."

"Yes." Bergman moved a connection. "It's the same principle of the wave I used to trap poor D an Mateo's ghost." H e paused and turned away, his eyes closed tightly. Then, regaining his composure, he said, "What I hope to do is to build a field—even a minor one will do—around this Eagle, so that whatever force is affecting John's vessel won't affect us."

"You think it important?"

H e said flatly, "John is no fool, H elena. H e isn maintaining radio silence because he wants to. A nd his controls aren't jammed from choice. H e's trapped and something has trapped him. Both of us have recogniz ed that."

A nd recogniz ed, too, that they in turn could be rendered as helpless as the commander. D oomed, as Koenig was doomed, to circle the O mphalos until their Eagle crashed to destructive ruin.

A nd for them there would be no rescue

From his chair Kano said, "We're getting close. You want to take over now?"

"Not yet, D avid." A lan Carter stared through the forward vision ports, narrowing his eyes against the green glow of the O mphalos, trying to see the minute shape of the Eagle against the convoluted mass. Before him an instrument clicked, clicked again, took up a repetitious buz z - ing.

"G ot it!" Kano stared at his own bank of in- struments. "The tracer has hooked on to the Commander's Eagle. D istance... velocity... direc- tion... " H e read out figures even as he was turning their own machine into a complementary path to the other. "If you're ready I'll—" H e broke off, blinking. "What's that? What the hell is it?"

Something huge, monstrous, rising on wings of lambent flame, eyes like mirrors of ice, jaws gap- ing wide enough to swallow them whole.

"The laser! Q uick!" Kano cried out as the thing engulfed them, seeing darkness as his senses swam and a giddiness turned his limbs to water. D ead, swallowed, made one with the great flying beast—the creature from nightmare. Why hadn't Carter fired? Why would he let them be killed?

"D avid!" H e heard the voice as from a great distance. "D avid! G et hold of yourself, man! D a- vid!"

Kano shuddered, seeing again the terrible shape of the Mbolnga bird, the frightful avenger which came to tear the living hearts from the guilty, to gulp down those who had run from bat- tle and hold them in its stomach, there to be pulped to a living, screaming jelly. O ld tales whis- pered to his great-grandfather in the flickering light of campfires, murmurs from reeded kraals, hints given by the tribal shamans with their devils' masks and mysterious powers.

How deep ran the racial heritage of mankind! "David!" Carter was anxious, his voice betraying his rising anger. "David, for God's sake, man!"

Kano said dully, "Didn't you see it?"

"See what?"

"A great bird. It came from nothing and—" He broke off, realizing that it was useless to explain. The thing had vanished as quickly as it had come. "Are we still tracking?"

"Yes." Carter checked the instruments with a practiced sweep of his eyes. "That bird you thought you saw. Was it—"

"Not thought," said Kano. "I did see it. To me, at least, it was real."

"All right. That bird you saw. Did it... " A blinked. In the co-pilot's seat a skeleton sat, grinning at him, hollow sockets for eyes, skeletal hands resting on the controls. Hands which moved as the head turned, the fleshless jaws gaping in the ghastly parody of a smile.

Death as his companion. Death in the Eagle Death at his side!

Tell-tales flared and alarms sounded as Carter tore at the controls, taking over from his co-pilot, the terrible figure which sat in menace at his side. Around him swirled a thin, green mist, blurring details, softening harsh outlines, seeming to cling to hands and head, face and hair, filling his lungs, thickening, solidifying, clogging... clogging...

And, abruptly, he was back in the sealed chamber where the aliens had died. His suit closed, the air gone, the enclosed space filled with

the taint of his own vomit. H e elt again the sick-
ening heaving of his lungs and stomach, the desperate need for air, to breathe, to escape.

A nd death, as before, was waiting.

D eath with its q uiet and subtle peace.

The warm and gentle darkness into which he
could sink and rest...   and rest.and rest...

A s Kano fought for their lives.

Carter had taken over full control and then had
seemingly gone to sleep. Kano slapped at the
switches, overrode the master control and re-
gained command. Beneath his hands the Eagle
was a horse running wild, a ship in a storm, a leaf
riding a whirlpool. L amps flashed their signals of
overstrained   systems,   guidance   mechanisms
fought opposing impulses, the stabiliz ers were at
war with themselves, the engines were blasting
against a reverse thrust, and even the life support
systems were flashing in the red.

Within moments circuits would blow as feed-
back current fused resistances and jumped gaps
never intended to handle such misapplied energies.

"D avid, your mask!" H e heard H elena's shout.
"The mask. Both of you use the mask!"

She was standing in the door leading back to
the passenger module, her face pale, and a smear
of blood running over her chin from a bitten lip. A
moment, then she had vanished, flung backwards
by the abrupt movement of the Eagle, a sudden
acceleration which drove Kano deep into his chair
and sent sparks flashing before his eyes.

A nother illusion or reality?

H ow could he tell?

H e groaned, fighting the pressure, tasting blood as his hand moved up towards the mask hanging below his mouth. The valve seemed to be stuck, the knob rejecting his fingers, and he groaned again as, with added desperation, he again attacked the metal. A year and the valve moved a little. A century and it opened a little more. A millennium and he smelled the stink of ammonia which rose to burn in his nostrils, to tingle in his lungs.

To wash his brain free of fantasy and to reveal the peril ahead.

The Eagle was plunging to utter destruction.

"A lan!" Kano yelled as he fought the controls. H e was a good pilot, trained, normally capable, but if the Eagle were to be saved now, they wanted not mere capability but a miracle. "A lan, for G od's sake!"

Before his eyes the signal lamps flared like the dancing of dust flecks on a stove. In the forward vision ports, the bulk of the O mphalos shone with a hungry, green glow, filling the area, the shadowed convolutions taking on the likeness of a mask, a grinning face, a waiting skull.

They were heading toward it too fast and at too steep an angle. A lready they must be below the orbit followed by the other Eagle. If dangerous fields were present, they had already entered them, and to escape would req uire skills perfected beyond the hampering need of thought. Carter had them; Kano knew he did not.

Freez ing the controls, he lunged towards the other man, gripped the valve of his mask, opened it, fell back into his seat just in time to prevent the Eagle from going into a long-ax is rotating spin.

"What?" Carter stirred. "What's the matter? What happened—Kano!"

"Take over, man! You wanted to come. You said you were the best, and now's your chance to prove it. Wake up, man!"

"I'm awake."

"Then take over." Kano hit a switch and folded his arms. "H ere! It's all yours. Now show us how good you are!"

There was nothing more *he* could do now.

t w el

O ce, when he had been very young, V ictor Bergman, had been taken by an uncle to a far land and there, at an ancient and holy place, had paid a coin to a fakir who had asked him what most he would like to be. The man had smiled when he had answered and had gently corrected the youthful aspirations. It was not enough, he said, to be rich and wise and famous. It was not even enough for a man to be clever. A bove all a man, any man, needed to be lucky.

Now, sitting in the Eagle, Bergman realiz ed again that, not for the first time, his luck had saved his life.

A gainst all odds Carter had managed to regain control. A gainst all logic the jumble of eq uipment he had assembled had, by sheer chance, formed connections which had produced the heterodyning field he had hoped would give protection. A nd H elena's compound had saved them from mind destroying hallucinations.

H unched in his seat he brooded over the stream of images, the false reality in which, for a space, he had been lost.

ROGUE PLANET

A vision of plumed horses, of crepe and solemn black, of mournful faces and mutes and bearers and armbands and hats dressed with ebony ribbons. A ll the pomp and panoply of a royal funeral. The ex aggerated respect paid to the dead King with doffed caps and bowed heads, of whispering voices, of ceremonial meals.

O f mourning ex tended.

O f grief maintained.

It was in his mind, all of it, memories and facts gathered when a boy, of the weight, of the customs of the time, of the heritage of the country to which his family had fled. The mystiq ue of death, caught, transported, used as a weapon against him, directed by his own subconscious to resemble a haven of peace.

A nd H elena?

She had been more wary than he, opening her valve before succumbing to the illusions, warned by her medical skill, sensitive to little signs of which he would have been unaware. A distortion of the light, perhaps, a slowness of thought or coordination.

"It worked," he said. "We've found a way to beat the O mphalos."

"Perhaps." She did not share his conviction. "A medical trick, V icto but we can't continue to inhale drugs. U nless we discontinue their use soon, the balance will have swung the other way and the anti-hallucinogens will produce distorting side-effects."

"Such as?" H e didn't really want to know. "Never mind. A s soon as we collect John we can get away from here. When will that be?"

A lan alone had the answer. A s Bergman and H elena stood in the doorway to the command module, he said, without turning in his chair, "We're now in orbit following a path a little higher than the other Eagle. We've reestablished the tracking monitor and have course and direction plotted. A ll that remains now is to go in."

"When?"

"It has to be soon. I'd like to take a few minutes to confirm relative courses and to establish any local patterns of variable turbulence. There could be magnetic fields, eddy currents, areas of contrasting potential."

"We didn't find any," reminded Bergman. "A ll sensors registered negative."

"They still do." Carter made a slight adjustment. "But I'd like to be sure. A s itsi, we won't have the chance."

The time factor, of course, Bergman had almost forgotten it.

"We have ten minutes," he said.

"We had." Carter was grim. "We haven't now. We used it up regaining control. You can give D avid the thanks for that," he added. "If it hadn't been for him, we'd all be dead now. If he ever gets tired of nursing his machine, he can transfer to R econnaissance any time he wants."

From Carter that was high praise and Kano beamed his gratification. But nothing, they all knew, would ever woo him away from the one great love of his life. To him the computer was more than a machine. It was an actual, living creature.

A nd one with a mellifluous, woman's voice.

"Is that John's Eagle?" H elena leaned forward as a fleck appeared on the screen. "There!"

It grew as they watched it, taking on shape and substance, a little vague against the greenish glow, the bulk of the O mphalos into which it was heading.

"Still no contact?"

"No, Professor." Kano checked his instruments. "We should be able to reach him but he doesn't answer." H e added, "A nd no contact with A lpha."

A s Bergman had ex pected. H is own heterodyning field which maintained the Eagle's systems from interference would also bolster the radio-barrier.

"We're going in," said Carter. "G et ready for the ex change. We'll have no time to waste so make it fast. Kano?"

"Five minutes total starting from—now!"

Five minutes in which to make actual physical contact with the other Eagle, to establish the seal, to enter and to carry Koenig back to safety. Bergman felt the deck of the Eagle move beneath his feet as he sealed his helmet. H elena had done the same and he stepped to where she was standing before the hatch and, counting seconds, waited.

Forty-three and the Eagle dipped, veered, shuddered as Carter fought to bring it into alignment with the other vessel.

Six tytwo and the clash of touching metal rang through the hull.

Eighty-seven and again the hulls touched, parted, touched again, the hulls clamped with the aid of powerful electromagnets. A boarding tube snaked out and make contact with the Koenig's Eagle. O nce the connection seal was firm, it q uickly began to pressuriz e.

"Contact established!" Carter signaled to Kano, now waiting in the passenger module. "D avid! G e moving!"

Three minutes in which to pass through the hatches, enter the other Eagle, get Koenig, return, seal, break apart and head away from the nearing danger of the O mphalos.

Kano went first, pushing impatiently past the sliding hatch and hurried through to the other Eagle with barely a glance at the boarding tube which joined the ships together. The ex ternal lock resisted did not respond to the keyed seq uence at first, and he pounded his weight against it, conscious of the passing seconds.

"H urry, D avid!" H elena's voice was straine tense as it came from his phones. "H urry!"

The lock yielded, the port opened and Kano rushed through the Eagle into the command module of Koenig's Eagle. The commander was slumped in his chair before the controls, head forward, face hidden by the fold of his arms.

"Two minutes!" said Carter. "H urry!"

"G et back in the Eagle, D octor R ussell!" snapped Kano, as she stepped towards the figure in the pilot's chair. "There's no time for you to treat him now. G et back and clear the way."

"H e could be hurt! L ifting him wrong could kill him!"

In answer to her concern, Kano reached to down to the instrument panel and turned off the artificial gravity. Moving him was a gamble they would have to take. A s she stepped back Kano moved to the chair, stooped, thrust his arms beneath the limp figure and lifted. Koenig sagged, one arm falling to trail across the back of the seat, his head almost hitting the edge of the port as Kano passed through it. H elena slammed it shut.

"Twelve seconds!" Carter's voice was brittle with tension. "H ve you got him safe?"

"Safe," said Bergman responded as Kano and H elena laid Koenig on the deck.

"G ood! Kano, break seal. Stand by for emergency lift. Now!"

The note of the engines rose, became a throbbing roar, ex haust gases blasting from the V enturis, as the Eagle tore free from the other vessel and began to lift from the danger below. For a moment it seemed as if they had waited too long, taken one chance too many. Then, as Kano stood waiting to retake the co-pilot's position, with a gusting sigh of relief, he saw the movement of needles, the shift of perspective.

"You've done it! Man, you've done it!"

Carter relax ed a little as the greenish bulk of the O mphalos dropped away. A gainst it the shape of the other vessel grew small, almost vanished, then suddenly ex panded in an eyesearing patch of raw and crimson flame.

"Three seconds," said Kano. "Three seconds more and we'd have shared that pyre." H e shuddered, then strapped into his seat across from Carter. H e said without turning, "Take a rest, A lan. I'll get us home from here."

Carter nodded, then without turning, he pressed a button for the intercom to the passenger module and asked, "H ow is the commander?"

There was no answer.

Koenig was lying where Bergman had placed him, face down, arms hiding his cheeks, his knees bent a little. H e looked a man asleep, only the steady rise and fall of his chest showing that he was still alive. H elena knelt and gently turned him over.

Bergman heard the sharp sound of her indrawn breath.

"H elena?"

"H is face," she whispered. "D ear G od, look at his face!"

It was old with an oldness which went beyond mere attrition of tissue. The lines were too deep, the skin too taut, the creped patches widespread so that he looked as a withered mummy might look, or a corpse which had been left to desiccate in some tropic sun.

It was the thing of her nightmares.

"John!" H elena threw back her helmet and stooped over him, her eyes wet with tears. "John!"

A call to the man she had known, the person with whom she had shared a fantastic adventure and perhaps a little more. Bergman saw her shoulders move in the unmistakable signs of grief and stood, feeling a little helpless, a little unwanted.

A nd he too felt grief.

They had wanted a miracle, and, for a brief moment, he had thought that one had been granted. The Eagle contacted, the hallucinations banished, the crippling stress-fields cancelled out and the commander saved. But saved for what?

"H e's dying!" said H elena. "D ying!"

Cursed by the age-accelerator which threatened the base. The sucking beam which drew life and energy from all it touched. Ellman had died because of it, and, even now, others might have succumbed. But no beam had impinged on the Eagle. Bergman said, "H elena. It might not be what think. The vapor—q uickly!"

"This isn't an hallucination, V ictor."

"To us, no, but to John?" H e left the q uestion hanging. "Try the vapor. Try it!"

Koenig coughed as she stripped the apparatus from around her neck and held the mask to his mouth and nose. H e stirred, one hand lifted as, weakly, he tried to push the device away.

"It isn't going to work," she said dully. "We've rescued him only to watch him die."

O f senescence, spending his last few days or hours like a crippled animal, his mind gone, his strength, his agility.

It would have been better to have left him to burn in the pyre of the fallen Eagle. A q uick and merciful death.

"H elena!" Bergman leaned forward from where he stood. "It's working. L ook!"

Koenig's face changed. The creped and desiccated skin began to smooth, the lines to fill, the corpse-like appearance to vanish. D ark circles remained around his eyes and his face still bore traces of age, but they were the result of fatigue, of muscles strained and settled into a mask of ex haustion.

"John!" H elena caught him as he coughed again and tried to stir. H is cheeks, Bergman noted, were moist with her tears. "John! O h, John!"

H is eyes opened and he stared at her with a blank ex pression. A man in a daz e, unbelieving that what he saw could be real. O ne who tried to smile and gasped and sucked vapor into his lungs and who, as they watched, became the man they had known and respected.

"H elena." Bergman dropped his hand to her shoulder. "H e'll be all right now. Just give him time to recover."

A nd to give herself time to gain composure, to adopt once more the iron mask of professional detachment.

But she could not forget what she had seen, the apparent miracle which had turned an old and dying man into one little older than herself and obviously fit.

"The vapor," she said. "It had to be that. But how did you know it would work?"

"I didn't," he confessed. "But now it seems obvious what must have happened. John was alone, unprotected, the victim of God-knows-what hallucinations. We both know the power of illusion. Under hypnosis a man can be convinced he cannot walk and he will be a literal cripple. Hysterical blindness, paralysis, loss of taste, of smell, of touch—you must have seen many cases."

"I have," she admitted, then added slowly, "So you are saying that John was suffering from a psychogenic condition?"

"What else?" Bergman paused, remembering his own experience. "He must have been subjected to intensely strong hallucinations formed of age and death, decay and collapse. Hallucinations so strong that they became an integral part of him and affected his actual physical being. Once convince the mind of a thing, and the body will follow. Drench it with the concept of age and the facial muscles will respond, the skin alter texture, the capillaries enlarge, the tissue show all the signs of desiccation. But, Helena, as a doctor you know all this."

She had known it, but had been too disturbed to look beyond the obvious. Bergman had done that, his mind relatively free of the emotions which had numbed her. The attribute of his mechanical heart, perhaps, or—

She shook her head, annoyed with the vein of calculation. What did it matter how he had arrived at the conclusion he had? H is suggestion had worked and Koenig was himself again.

H e smiled as again she leaned over him.

"H elena! A re you real?"

"Yes, John. I'm real."

"You came after me," he said slowly. "R escued me." H is eyes moved from the woman to where Bergman stood silently watching. "You and V ictor and who else?" H e frowned as she told him. "A nd what if you had been trapped as I was?"

"Nothing." She met his eyes. "V ictor left orders that under no circumstances was a second rescue attempt to be made."

She, all of them, had taken a calculated gamble with death but there was nothing he could say. The decision had been a personal one and he would have done exactly the same. O ne attempt could be justified—more could not. A lpha could not afford to waste crews and Eagles.

A s he climbed to his feet to stand unsteadily, one hand supporting his weight, Bergman said, "You were locked in orbit around the O mphalos, John. You had time to study it. D id you—"

"D ecide what it was?" Koenig shrugged. "I only know one thing, V ictor. It is inimical—and it is alive."

A live in a way in which nothing in his ex perience had been alive. A node of awareness, self contained, a mesh of balanced energies forming a living, conscious world. A nd it was conscious, of that he had no doubt. Sitting in the passenger compartment of the Eagle, eyes half-closed, he recalled and relived that dreadful time during which the entire universe had been filled with the desire and the concept of death.

"It's sentient," he ex plained. "A form of life which we can only understand by analogy. Think of an oyster or a barnacle. A plant such as a V e-nus flytrap. A sea urchin, a leech, a basking whale. The O mphalossi all of these and more. You called it a brain, H elena. It is that too."

"A conscious brain?" Bergman was fast with the q uestion. "A re the beams directed against the Moon and the planetoid the result of a conscious decision?"

"Intelligent direction, John?" H elena frowned. "Is it possible?"

H e said dully, conscious of the inability of mere words to convey what he had felt, "Perhaps not intelligent as we use the term. Those beams could have been emitted as we would put out a hand to touch something. O r as a parasite would automat-ically introduce a proboscis into the skin of a vic-tim. It reacted to our presence. Perhaps it couldn't help but to react. It, like ourselves, like all living things, is driven by the need to survive. To it, we are little more than a source of energy."

Food!

H elena looked at where the O mphalos was pic-tured on a screen to the fore of the compartment.

It was smaller now they were on their way back to A lpha. Carter, she noticed had, with innate caution, taken a flight path which kept them well clear of the energy-sucking cone.

Even as she watched, the green ex panse seemed to flex with its mysterious pulsations.

A creature born in an alien dimension stirring at the impact of intelligent life?

R esponding to mental stimuli, received per-haps at a paraphysical level?

A nd if the thing were sleeping and should wake—what then?

The concept chilled her, then she shook her-self, aware of her flight into fantasy, the sudden flurry of an undisciplined imagination. It was a relief to listen to what Bergman was saying.

"John, you said that to the O mphalos we were little more than a source of energy. That is, a source of food. D o you imply that we could be even more?"

A moment in which Koenig remained silent, looking ahead with haunted eyes, aware of the trap into which his private knowledge had led him. The impression he had gained of something into which other sentient creatures could and had been assimilated. O f a plethora of minds aware and helplessly entrammeled. O f the ghostly ech-oes of screams.

"Perhaps," he said at last. A nd then to change the subject, "D id you manage to measure the rate of attrition on the planetoid?"

"Not to the precision I would like, John, but we took some rough measurements. It is slow as I anticipated. We seem to be dealing with a total conversion of matter into energy and there must be a limiting factor to the amount which can be stored and utiliz ed." H e added grimly, "But there's no danger of the thing going hungry for a long time yet. The mass of the Moon alone will keep it supplied for millennia."

The rock, the dust and stone. The minerals and chemicals and deposits. The people too, but Koenig didn't want to think of that.

H elena pressed him back in the seat as he at- tempted to rise.

"Take it easy, John. There's nothing for you to do now."

"I want to see if we can contact the base."

"Why?" She frowned as he made no answer. "The defense shield? Paul has kept it on as you ordered. A nything else?"

"The metal we found," he said. "The olive stuff lining the tunnel sand chamber of the aliens. D id you find out what it was, V ictor?"

"Basically, some form of non-ferrous alloy aligned to long-chain polymers of a silicone struc- ture. They must have found a way to blend the various materials into a flux which they spread and let harden as we do with an epox y glue. O nce set, it's difficult to cut and impossible to rework."

"Can we duplicate it?"

"Not at the moment and I doubt if we will ever be able to match it ex actly." Bergman rubbed thoughtfully at his chin. "I didn't have much time to work on it myself, but Sarah Pulcher is doing her best. She knows metals and plastics better than any, John. If there's an answer to be found, then she'll find it."

Koenig nodded, remembering the woman, a talkative and insistent person. She'd been an annoying thorn in his in the weeks leading up to the play, but he'd never doubted her professional q ualifications and skill. She was an important asset to his staff. H e made a mental note to remind her of it.

H elena said, "Why the interest, John? What importance can the alien metal have for us?"

"Those creatures used it for protection," he ex plained. "They lined their tunnels and chamber with it."

"Naturally, so as to seal them against air loss." She saw his eyes, his ex pression. "But you think there was something else, John. A protection against what?" H er mind leapt to the answer. "The aging element of the energy-beam? Is that it?"

"I don't know. It was only a possibility."

"We could make a test." H elena frowned, thinking. "Culture plates," she decided. "Bob is already working with them. Pulcher could shield them with some of the alien metal and see if there is any change in the catabolic rate."

"See if the radio is working. If it is, give the orders."

Koenig tried to relax as she left, knowing there was nothing more he could do for the present. If contact could be established, then everything possible for the moment would have been done.

In the meantime, it was good just to sit, to know he was safe among his fellows, that the ghastly isolation he had known when orbiting the O mphalos was a thing of the past.

Something to be forgotten—if such a thing could ever be.

t h i r t e

Koenig was exhausted, but he had no time to rest. They were running against the clock now. He sat on the divan in Helena's office-she beside him. He rested his head in his hands. Helena could see how utterly spent he was. It worried her, but there was nothing she could do for him at the moment.

Koenig turned to look at her and said, "Tell me about Sanderson. How is he doing?"

"He's in a subsurface medical unit we've set up. I've taken him off electro-sleep and he is recovering, with just enough sedation to keep him calm."

"What do you think drove him to attempt suicide?" Koenig asked.

Helena said, "If you are asking me whether Greg Sanderson is suicidal—I'd say no. Everyone has reacted differently to the successive terror fields we've passed through. Some people more than others. I think the combination of cabin fever, pain killers and alcohol—compounded by the effects of the terror field—pushed him to try to escape. I don't think he was consciously suicidal. That's my professional opinion."

"So, you are saying I shouldn't let it affect his duty assignment when this is all over?"

"Not unless some other indication of emotional instability shows itself. You know how much he values his position and his freedom. D o you want to take those away from him?"

"O f course not, H elena. I just need to know he won't be a danger to himself... or others."

"L et's see how it goes, John. You owe him that much," H elena reminded him.

Koenig nodded then rose as the door to H elena's office slid open and Sarah Pulcher and Bob Mathias took their places before him, waiting to present their latest respective updates.

Koenig turned first to Pulcher and asked, "Were we even on the right track? Can the alien metal give protection?"

"No." She pulled out a folder and checked the notations. "D o you want the details? O ver a grand total of twenty-three tests the figures are—"

"Never mind the figures, Sarah. In your opinion to continue working with the metal for that object is to waste time. R ight?"

She nodded. "Yes, Commander. If the aliens used it to block the aging process, then their metabolism must have been far different from our own."

"Mathias?"

"I concur. It provided no protection I could detect," he said.

Koenig considered for a moment. "Thank you, Sarah," he said thoughtfully. "You've been most helpful."

She took that as her cue to leave, and Helena waited until the door had shut behind her before she asked, "Are there any new casalties, Bob?"

"Two, neither fatal." He gestured towards the intensive care unit. "Nyat Cheng and Ivan Cernik. Both outside workers."

"Treatment?"

"Complete blood-changes, massive injections of hormones, drips of saline and glucose, marrow implants to restore red corpuscle production, anti-calcium treatment and wide-range antibiotics injected at freq uent intervals." Mathias made a helpless gesture. "I don't think anything we can try will work completely. If it did, we'd have made an advance in geriatrics. The most we can hope for is to arrest the progress of the effects of the beam. They are now in a deep shelter. But, Helena, I think that they'll have lost a good ten years off their life ex pectancy. I don't think there's anything I can do to give that back to them or to stave off the inevitable."

"There is to be no further work on the surface," said Koenig. "A ll personnel restricted to base and all non-essential workers to be kept confined to the lower levels. Those working close to the outside to be rotated at freq uent intervals." He snatched the commlock from his belt. "V ictor?"

Bergman stared from the tiny screen.

"What is it, John?"

ROGUE PLANET

"A n emergency conference in my office in ten minutes. Bring all available data on the present situation, with special emphasis on the rate of energy flow from targets to main body." Koenig pressed a button. "Conway?"

"H ere, Commander."

"A djust all atomic piles to the max imum production of plutonium."

"A ll?" The nuclear engineer looked startled. "R emember the storage problems, Commander."

"A ll," said Koenig. "U se automation and take risks with the non-essential eq uipment if you must, but I want top production."

A s he pressed another button, H elena said, "What's in your mind, John?"

"Survival."

"By producing plutonium?" She blinked as, ignoring the q uestion, he relayed a stream of orders to other sections of the base. "John! What are you doing?"

"Come to the conference," he snapped. "A nd find out."

It was a meeting dominated by one man, and she realiz ed that, subconsciously, he had made his decision long before, taking his place at the round conference table. The doors were closed but, beyond, in Main Mission, the instruments were watching their common enemy. The green, brain-like mass of the O mphalos. The enigmatic thing which held them trapped, which was sucking away energy and life, which had to be destroyed.

A s Koenig emphasiz ed the point, she realiz ed that she had ex pected it. H ad even accepted it. Bergman alone was dubious.

"If, as you say, it has rudimentary awareness, John, then destroying it without regard would be in the nature of an immoral act. H ave we the right to use violence? Must life always be gained at the ex pense of another's?"

Koenig said slowly, "V ictor, we have no choice. Men are dead and dying because of it. The aliens were wiped out. No one knows how many other life-forms and races have been destroyed by that thing. It is killing us and, to save ourselves, we must render it harmless. I am willing to listen to any other feasible alternative. You have one?"

"Can we communicate with it in some way?" Joan Conway from the Nuclear G enerating Plant ran her hand through her hair. "H ave we tried?"

"Yes."

"Without success?"

"I've been in touch with it as close as I believe any intelligent creature can be." Koenig's face hardened as he remembered the seeming eternity of loneliness, the numbing pressure of all things associated with death, the deaths he had mentally ex perienced, the hunger he had sensed, the ferocity. "I don't know if we can call it alive as we use the term. Perhaps it is nothing more than a reactive device, the result of an ex periment perhaps, something which lies beyond our knowledge and previous ex perience. But I do know, and know it with every fiber of my being, that unless we destroy it, it will destroy us. To me the choice is simple. V ictor?"

"A s you say, John."

"H elena?"

"I agree."

Conway said, before she asked, "The safety of A lpha comes first, Commander—but can we destroy it? Can we even hurt it?"

"I think we can." Koenig glanced at Bergman. "You have the figures, V ictor. We know the energy potential available to us. If we use it correctly, we have a chance." H e ended bleakly, "It's the only one we have."

A lan Carter had been the first to volunteer. Now he sat at the controls of the Eagle on the launching pad, watching the brilliant display in his screens. The defense shield arching over him was a dome of scintillate rainbows, sparkling, coruscating, heart-stoppingly beautiful. It would, he hoped, protect him from becoming prematurely old. Bergman had said that it would, that the balance of energies now achieved would, at least, stave off the fate suffered by Ellman. That he would not end on a cot as Cheng and Cernik had done. Now three others had taken their place.

The last, he hoped, and had justification. They had worked on the surface. Since the ban no other cases had been reported.

"R eady, A lan?"

Paul Morrow talking from the screen. Carter nodded, then said, "R eady when you are."

"R ight. O n five. Mark!" H is voice held no ex pression as he gave the count. "Z ero. Now!"

The screen died and, as it did, the engines of the Eagle flared to full power, the vessel rising to swing out and away from the danger of the cone, the defense shield glowing again as soon as the area was clear. A system designed to gain max imum protection and one, they all hoped, which would do just that.

O n the planetoid, Koenig watched as the Eagle landed. H e stood on the smooth, curved surface, some distance from the shaft they had found, the ground all around littered with stacked box e and eq uipment. Two other Eagles were grounded to one side and, as Carter's vessel landed, one of them lifted and headed back toward the Moon.

"A ndrews?" Koenig spoke into his radio. "Is that you?"

"Yes, Commander."

"R emember to hand over to Fraser when you arrive. You've done three flights and that's enough."

"I can manage, Commander."

"You'll do as I order!" Koenig made no attempt to soften his tone. "If you want to gain fifty years in a few minutes that's your concern. I'm worried about the Eagle. If you want to be a hero then do it without risking the ship. U nderstood?"

"Commander, I—"

"You're a fool," Koenig interrupted. Then add- ed more softly, "A nd A lpha needs all the fools like you it can get. I don't want to waste one. You've served your stint, man. G et back, put Fraser in charge of the Eagle and report to Medical for checking. No arguments now. D o it!"

H e turned as the Eagle vanished from sight and stepped towards the head of the shaft. O n all sides, men were busy moving the crates, handling them with ex aggerated care, never placing them too close to each other. A t the head of the shaft, technicians emptied the box es and handed their contents down to others who moved them along the tunnels.

They had worked for hours like a horde of busy ants shifting scraps of leaves to form an underground farm. But these things they carried were not leaves and they would build no farm. D own in the chamber which held the dead aliens, buried deep beneath the surface and sealed by the stubborn metal, a tremendous bomb was in process of manufacture.

A fission bomb which would emulate the sun in its fury.

"John?" Bergman climbed slowly from the shaft rising up a metal ladder which had made progress easier than the original hoops. H is voice was fatigued, the way he moved betrayed his tiredness, the way he stood.

"H ow's it going?"

"Well, but—"

"Follow me. L et's get into Torens's Eagle and take a break. You could do with some coffee."

"I can manage."

"You too?" Koenig grunted his irritation. "The place is swarming with craz yidiots who want to work themselves to death. Come and get some coffee, V ictor. That's an order."

O ne that Bergman was glad to obey. L ater, sitting in the Eagle with a steaming cup of coffee in his hand, he admitted that he was tired.

"I'm not surprised," said Koenig. "H ow long has it been since you last slept?"

"A bout as long as you've been awake, John."

"Which makes us two of a kind." Koenig took a sip of his own coffee. "H ow much longer will it be?"

H e was talking of the bomb and Bergman knew it. H e said,"We've almost got everything into place down below. The initial fission device is set and now we're arranging the rest. It's a big charge, John."

"It needs to be."

"But not big enough to volatiz e this planetoid."

Koenig said impatiently, "I know that, V ictor, but it doesn't have to. You worked out the figures and decided on the megaton scale necessary. It's close but it will have to do."

"I'd like another two loads set in place just to make sure." Bergman produced his inevitable slide rule and manipulated it, forgetting his coffee in his sudden introspection. "Two loads at least," he decided. "There are too many variables which we haven't been able to take into full account. The core, for ex ample. It could be of unsuspected density."

"We'll have to use what we've got, V ictor."

"But, John—"

"We have no choice. D id you know that three more have fallen from age sickness?"

"I know, but the defense shield will prevent further cases."

"A s far as we know but how can we be sure? The power may fail, the energy-beam take more than we can deliver, circumstances may change at any moment. We've got to act while we have the chance."

R ising, Koenig paced the confines of the passenger module. H ow to ex plain the fear which engulfed him? The conviction that already they were on borrowed time?

"Commander!" Torens called from the command module. "The O mphalos come and look!"

It hung in space as he remembered, greenly glowing, marked with the dark tracery of lines which gave the appearance of convolutions, divided into the resemblance of a human brain.

A nd then it pulsed.

"John!" Bergman leaned towards the screen. "It— It—"

H ow to describe the sudden inflation and deflation of apparently solid matter? The previously noted pulsations had been minor, the product of an interplay of light or the interpretation of a daz - z led mind. But this had been no gentle undulation.

"G od!" Torens was a man with no concept of personal fear but now his voice held a strained terror. "It moved! Commander—the damn thing's alive!"

The drugs were bitter to the taste, tablets which he swallowed and washed down with a sickly liq - uid. D ope to keep him awake and aware, to force tired muscles to respond, eyes to see, his brain to think.

"John, you shouldn't take all these things." H elena had been reluctant to give them, yielding only to his direct order, his thinly veiled anger at her reluctance to obey. "You'll pay for this later."

"Sure—now don't bother me."

"John—"

"H elena, we're fighting time. G ive what drugs are needed and spare me your lectures. D on't you understand? We're fighting for our lives!"

A gainst a thing which could not ex ist but, incredibly, did.

Koenig stared at it where it rested in the screens. A round him in Main Mission, everyone seemed to be holding their breath, waiting, standing posed on the brink of ex tinction.

"The O mphalos has increased its previous siz e by twenty percent," Morrow reported. "and is now pulsing at twice the rate observed at commencement."

"Sandra?"

"Energy loss mounting, Commander. The rate is nearing totality."

Complete absorption, the energy drained as fast as it was produced, and when the defense shield went down all would be helplessly ex posed to the aging action of the alien forces.

Time!

It was running against them, wasted by neces- sity, precious seconds turning into minutes, into hours.

H ow much longer did they have?

"What news from the Eagle, Paul?"

"O n its way, Commander. A ll remaining per- sonnel aboard together with Professor Bergman."

"H ave him report here as soon as he docks. G et me Weapons Section." Koenig waited as an aux iliary screen blurred to steady, to picture the taut face of a Weapons Chief Petrov.

"Commander?"

"R eport on readiness for action."

"A ll as ordered. Tubes aimed and ready. Mis- siles primed and all warheads with treble charg- es." H esitating, he added, If we fire as ordered we'll be stripped of all capability."

"If you don't, we'll be dead."

Koenig shook his head as the screen darkened. Too many drugs taken too q uickly had fogged his vision and etched at his self-control, but he'd had no choice and neither had the others. Morrow, red-eyed, face slack with weariness. Sandra, look- ing like a ghost, Kano a grim and silent figure, H elena reproachful, and yet helpless to do more than what she had done.

A nd now she could do nothing but wait.

Wait as Carter's Eagle came into view, darting in to land as the screen lowered, settling as again the shield lifted, the lights dimming, almost dying, restored as Morrow adjusted his instruments.

Close—and the shield had lost its previous brilliance. Even now she could be growing old with accelerated speed, bones becoming brittle, blood thinning, glands withering, life and the lust for life drained and sucked by the alien thing to which this constricted universe belonged.

H ow long had it traversed space?

A tiny thing at the beginning, perhaps, feeding on energy, growing, developing, aware of food sources, catching them with its beams, reducing them into energy which it stole. Eating them.

A roving parasite of the void.

A danger sealed into a place of its own by some race owning a tremendously high technology but lacking the inclination to destroy. Instead, they had warped the very fabric of the continuum to form an escape-proof cage and had set it about with warnings of what it contained and concentric fields of abject terror.

"V ictor!" Koenig turned as Bergman entered Main Mission and came toward him. "Is everything ready?"

"Yes." Bergman glanced at the chronometer. "Firing commences in one hour thirty-three minutes."

"So long?"

"The planetoid must be in the right position for the plan to work. Computer gave position and timing. R ight, D avid?"

"Yes, Professor." Kano rubbed at his reddened eyes. "A ny deviation from the plan will result in lost efficiency."

A lowering of the already slim margin of potential success, but the odds against them were growing all the time. Koenig glanced at the dials, saw the needles edging toward the red, the warning flash of signal lights.

"Cut all unessential power to all areas, Paul."

"I've saved all I can, Commander."

"Save more. Switch to emergency battery power if you have to. Just remember that we'll need full power fed into the shield when we blow."

Morrow acknowledged with a nod and Koenig moved to where H elena stood watching the screens. The greenish light, now a blaz ing flame, touched her face and accentuated the strong contours of jaw and cheeks, the wide set of the eyes.

She whispered, "That pulsing, John. It's like the pounding of a heart."

O r the kick of a child impatient to be born. Yet how could familiar concepts apply? The O mphalos was not a creature giving birth, nor yet a creature being born. It was ex panding, growing as an organic thing would grow, and yet it was not organic.

Koenig remembered the sensations he had ex - perienced, when lost in the illusions he had known while in close prox imity to the green bulk. H ad he ex perienced the stored knowledge of actual beings? The deaths—had they been actual memories of minds absorbed by the O mphalos?

A germ, he thought, caught in a human bloodstream, drawn to the brain, entrammeled in the cortex , sharing, in part, the stir and process of thought.

D id a man consider the fate of what he ate?

Would he care if it was aware?

"Thirteen minutes, Commander." Sandra Benes was tense, uneasily aware of the superstition connected to the number. Now, if at all, any bad luck would surely become manifest. D espite her resolution not to look she lifted her eyes to where the main screen depicted the O mphalos. It was twice its original siz e now, pulsating, greenly malevolent. A predator poised and ready to strik. A bomb on the edge of ex plosion.

"Sandra!"

Morrow had been watching her and at the sound of his voice she started, dropping her eyes from the hypnotic image, concentrating again on her instruments.

"Sorry, Paul."

"Time?"

"Eleven minutes." A t least the unlucky number had been safely passed. "Energy loss mounting. Some traces of temperature differential noted from the central body."

"H igh?" Bergman fired the q uestion.

"No. It's varying from z ero to twelve degrees Celsius."

"A ny radiation?"

"Slight traces, Professor, but our own energy loss is affecting the readings."

"But they are positive?"

Bergman grunted as she nodded. To Koenig he said, "You realiz e what this means, John? The ex ternal layers of the O mphalos must be splitting. The result, perhaps, of the massive increase in its energy intake since we entered its space. It is obviously adapting to meet the new circumstances."

"G rowing?"

"In a sense, John, yes. A s a crystal will grow when immersed in a super-saturated solution. It is a sponge absorbing energy, using it to build up its mass, adding to its reserves. L ater, if all sources of energy should be denied to it, then the reverse process will apply. It will shrink as it consumes its own bulk. Men do the same, John. A nd stars. It seems to be a universal law."

Eat or starve.

G row or wither.

Kill or die!

Koenig glanced at the screens, the instruments facing Morrow where he sat, the tell-tales and monitors of the console. The base was on R ed A lert, ground defenses standing by, engineers ready to wring the last erg of power from all generators and to maintain a max imum flow no matter what the cost.

"Three minutes." Sandra's voice betrayed her strain. "Two and a half. Two."

Now only a hundred seconds to wait...   ninety... eighty...   seventy...

Koenig felt H elena at its side and turned his head to smile reassurance.

"Soon now."

"John! If it doesn't work!"

"It will! It must!"

Their only chance and if it failed, death would be waiting. A   gamble with their lives as the stake.

"Ten!" Sandra began to count the seconds. A t the console Morrow sent signals to the waiting men. Bergman, eyes narrowed, stared at the glowing mass of the O mphalos. Kano gently stroked a panel as if giving comfort to his beloved computer.

Koenig felt his face harden and grow wet with ooz ing sweat.

H had to be right.

H ad to!

"Three...   Two...   O ne...   Now!" A   moment, Sandra said bleakly, "It isn't working. It isn't going to work!"

"Wait!" Bergman turned from the screen. "We can't see anything as yet and your instruments can't pick up what lies behind the O mphalos. Paul?"

"Booster signals sent, Professor, but the automatics should have fired by now."

The time fuses planted with the massed nuclear materials in the body of the planetoid. H eaped in mathematical precision in the chamber of alien dead. A tremendus bomb which flashed to life in an eye-searing halo about the O mphalos.

A wide circle of savage, bluewhite glare which dulled the green. Which spread to form a backdrop of sun-like fury.

"It worked!" Bergman shouted his relief. "John! It worked!"

The fuses, yes. The nuclear bomb itself, yes. But the rest?

A flood of raw radiation, by itself, wouldn't have been enough. The O mphalos ate energy, it used it, lived on it, sucked it in. A t the distance, savage though it was, the atomic ex plosion would have been of limited use. But there had been more.

The planetoid with its shafts and mass. The chamber which had held the bomb, the blasting ex plosion which had torn the remnants of what had once been an inhabited world apart, fragments which even now, if the calculations had been correct, were hurtling towards the green menace.

A blast of matter which would rip into the O mphalos with the impact of a shotgun blast against a bag of water.

Matter which would be converted into energy on contact, each grain of dust, every fragment in turn an atomic ex plosion.

"Paul! Fire all missiles!"

Morrow nodded at Koenig's command and relayed the order. From the launching tubes ringing the base, slender shapes lanced into space, torpedoes loaded with a treble charge of atomic destruction in their heads, their drive mechanisms rigged to gain max imum velocity at the ex pense of accuracy.

The target was too big to be missed.

Morrow said anx iously, "Commander! The shield?"

"Wait!"

There was time yet and every second was precious. Koenig stood, mentally counting, visualiz ing what was happening in space. The flight of the massed torpedoes, the paths taken by the masses torn from the disrupted planetoid. They would strike together, a double blow in opposed syn chroniz ation and, when they did,the O mphalos would die.

The alien mass would be destroyed, disintegrated, bathed with a flood of energy so intense that it could not be stored or utiliz ed.

"Commander?"

"Not yet."

"But, John!" Bergman too was anx ious. "If—"

"Wait!"

A knifeedged calculation. R aise the defense shield to full strength too soon, and the energy would be drained to leave them defenseless against the moment of need. Wait too long, and they too would be blasted by the flood of raw destruction soon to fill the enclosed area of this miniature universe.

ROGUE PLANET

O n the screen the O mphalos flickered, seemed to jerk, to swell, to ex pand with frightening speed.

"Now, Paul! Now!"

The blaz e of the defense shield matched the fury of the heavens, the daz z le of scintillating particles blasting the eyes with a mass of kaleidoscopic coruscations.

For a long moment there was silence, then H elena said, "John, is it holding?"

"Sandra?"

"Energy loss mounting towards total drain. Still climbing." H er voice q uivered a little and the knuckles of her hands where they gripped the edge of the panel shone white. "Climbing. Climbing—no, steadying now. Steady and falling. Falling! Commander—we are safe!"

Safe behind the protection of the shield as the naked fury of disrupted atoms streamed around them, filling all space with a maelstrom of tormented energies, stresses mounting, conflicting, tearing at the very fabric of the continuum until something had to yield.

When it did, it was like the snapping of an overstrained rubber band.

Koenig felt a jerk, a sudden movement of the floor beneath his feet, a shudder which ran through the base, then heard Bergman's startled cry.

"L ook! The stars! The stars!"

The screen was full of them, bright, coldly remote but comforting in their familiarity. Space was normal again, the bubble which had held them prisoner broken and dissolved.

They were free. O f the O mphalos, nothing re mained but a dying smear of fading emerald—the pyre of a destroyed world.

ROGUE PLANET

From the Journal of Commander John Koenig:

Our recent experience with the Omphalos brought us to edge of destruction. The Omphalos was alive and perilous to all who crossed its devastating path, feeding on the matter, energy and the souls of all those it consumed. I can only hope that by destroying it, we helped to liberate those uncounted beings who were trapped within it – or, at least, bring an end to their suffering.

However, the struggle to free ourselves from the pocket universe of the Omphalos was not the only one we faced. Its insidious attack racked not only our bodies but our minds, each of us forced to confront our inner fears and insecurities. I was not immune from its mental assault, and I know that its avenue of attack on my mind came from within me. My own doubts. My survival is wholly due to the efforts and determination of my fellow Alphans.

I am left with the memories of those moments in communion with the Omphalos.

In the years since the Moon was blasted out of Earth's orbit, Alpha has plunged though a hostile universe. As commander, I have keenly felt the weight of responsibility and done my best to ensure the survival of my people, perhaps even of the human race.

The Omphalos shone a light on my fear that I may have failed them.

Since September 13th 1999, tens of Alphans have died. I am ashamed to write that I don't know the exact count at this moment. I've spoken at more memorial services than any other commander of Moonbase Alpha, and, at each, I wonder, what more could I have done?

Among the burdens of command is sadness. Alpha is a small community and each loss is increasingly a personal one. But as commander, I have a unique responsibility for every life, and every death. I now find myself wrestling with the accusations of the Omphalos – drawn from my own thoughts – as to my culpability in all those deaths.

The hardest thing is knowing not that I failed them through some lack of will or competence, but that I was unable to save them despite my best efforts.

Ultimately, I have come to believe that there are no guarantees. There are no second chances in space. It is a harsh and unforgiving realm, and our survival will always be at risk. Self-doubt and self-pity are a recipe for failure.

As I look at the blue-white star of the planetary system we are approaching, I am filled with renewed hope. Perhaps there we will find a world on which to settle, to live again as human beings.

ROGUE PLANET

And even if we are met with disappointment and adversity once again, we will overcome it. Our struggle will continue.

So, I look to the future without expectations but with optimism, and I put aside my doubts and recriminations.

The rest is silence.

About the Author

Edwin Charles Tubb was a British writer of science fiction, fantasy and western novels. The author of over 140 novels and 230 short stories and novellas, Tubb is best known for The Dumarest Saga, an epic science-fiction saga set in the far future. Michael Moorcock wrote, "His reputation for fast-moving and colourful SF writing is unmatched by anyone in Britain." Among numerous science fiction novels, E.C. Tubb is the author of many of the classic novelizations of *Space:1999* episodes as well as the original novels *Alien Seed*, *Rogue Planet* and *Earthfall*.